AMERICAN POETS PROJECT

AMERICAN POETS PROJECT

IS PUBLISHED WITH A GIFT IN MEMORY OF

James Merrill

AND SUPPORT FROM ITS FOUNDING PATRONS

Sidney J. Weinberg, Jr. Foundation

The Berkley Foundation

Richard B. Fisher and Jeanne Donovan Fisher

The Essential
Gwendolyn
Brooks

elizabeth alexander editor

AMERICAN POETS PROJECT

THE LIBRARY OF AMERICA

Published in the United States by Library of America.
Visit our website at www.loa.org.

This paper exceeds the requirements of ANSI Z39.48–1992 (Permanence of Paper).

Design by Chip Kidd and Mark Melnick.
Frontispiece: Gwendolyn Brooks, ca. 1972; © Bettmann/CORBIS

Library of Congress Cataloging-in-Publication Data:
Brooks, Gwendolyn, 1917–2000.
  [Poems. Selections]
  The Essential Gwendolyn Brooks ; Elizabeth Alexander, editor.
      p. cm. — (American poets project ; 19)
      ISBN 978-1-931082-87-7 (alk. paper)
    I. Alexander, Elizabeth, 1962– II. Title. III. Series.

PS3503.R7244A6 2005
811'.54— dc22

                                                              2005044162

10 9 8 7 6 5

Gwendolyn Brooks

CONTENTS

INTRODUCTION

Since she began publishing her tight lyrics of Chicago's great South Side in the 1940s, Gwendolyn Brooks has been one of the most influential American poets of the twentieth century. Her poems distill the very best aspects of Modernist style with the sounds and shapes of various African-American forms and idioms. Brooks is a consummate portraitist who found worlds in the community she wrote out of, and her innovations as a sonneteer remain an inspiration to more than one generation of poets who have come after her. Her career as a whole also offers an example of an artist who was willing to respond and evolve in the face of the dramatic historical, political, and aesthetic changes and challenges she lived through.

Gwendolyn Elizabeth Brooks was born in 1917 in Topeka, Kansas, the daughter of Keziah Wims Brooks and David Anderson Brooks. Her father aspired to be a doctor and studied medicine for a year and a half at Fisk, but ended up working as a janitor. He was the son of a runaway slave. Her mother was a teacher before her marriage and then turned her full attention to homemaking, attending fiercely to the creative talent of young Gwendolyn from an early age. Her mother would tell her that she was going to be "the *lady* Paul Laurence Dunbar." The family moved to Chicago shortly after Brooks's birth, and she would spend the rest of her life on that city's South Side—a great "Negro metropolis"—through years when the innovation, strength, struggle, and vision of its black residents gave her a backdrop and context for all that would interest her in her work.

The Chicago of Brooks's formative years bustled with creative and political energy. Black Southern migrants from the second wave of the Great Migration flocked to the city in large numbers. In 1936, Harlem was the only neighborhood in the United States with a larger black population than Chicago's South Side. For many of the Chicago characters in Brooks's poems, as well as its real-life residents, the rural South was close at hand in memory and ways even as people navigated the rough and ready wind-whipped city. The South represented the beauty of home ways, but it was also the economically, spiritually, and physically violent home of white supremacy.

In 1935, the WPA Federal Writers' Project began, and Chicago was a hive of subsidized artistic activity that often dovetailed with progressive interracial (if problematically so) political movements. More artists participated in the Federal Writers' Project in Chicago than in any other city in the United States. In 1936, the novelist Richard Wright formed the South Side Writers group that included poets Frank Marshall Davis and Margaret Walker, playwright Theodore Ward, and the admired poet-critic Edward Bland, who died in World War II and whom Brooks memorialized in a poem. In the flourishing years from 1935 to the end of World War II, Chicago was home at various times to a collection of creative people that rivaled the

Harlem Renaissance. There were artists such as Charles Sebree, Eldzier Cortor, Charles White, Elizabeth Catlett, Gordon Parks, Hughie Lee-Smith, Archibald Motley, and writers such as Wright, Walker, Davis, Fenton Johnson, Margaret Cunningham Danner, Margaret Burroughs, Bernard Goss, Arna Bontemps, Frank Yerby, Marita Bonner, and Willard Motley. Dancer Katherine Dunham was finishing her studies in anthropology at the University of Chicago. Paul Robeson and Langston Hughes would frequently pass through and connect with that crowd. Claude McKay attended the publication party for Brooks's first book. In the first installment of her autobiography, *Report From Part One*, Brooks describes the exciting social life that she and her husband, Henry, enjoyed in the early 1940s:

> My husband and I knew writers, knew painters, knew pianists and dancers and actresses, knew photographers galore. There were always weekend parties to be attended where we merry Bronzevillians could find each other and earnestly philosophize sometimes on into the dawn, over martinis and Scotch and coffee and an ample buffet. Great social decisions were reached. Great solutions for great problems were provided. . . . Of course, in that time, it was believed, still, that the society could be prettied, quieted, cradled, sweetened, if only people talked enough, glared at each other yearningly enough, waited enough.

The black press was also a powerful force. John Sengstacke was building the *Chicago Defender* into the most noted black paper in the country, where one could regularly read cutting-edge political news, poetry, and the column by Langston Hughes which began in 1942. John Johnson, who went on to found and publish *Jet*, *Ebony*, *Sepia*, and *Negro*

Digest/Black World, under the aegis of his Johnson Publications, was in a writers' group with Brooks.

Brooks attended junior college, began working, and soon married Henry Blakely, who was also a poet. They were both intensely devoted to their work, though like most poets they did other work for money. Their first child, Henry Jr., was born in 1940. In 1941, Brooks joined a poetry workshop organized by a wealthy white woman, Inez Cunningham Stark, who had been the president of the Renaissance Society at the University of Chicago and had helped bring the likes of Leger, Prokofiev, and Le Corbusier to the city. Stark also had a long affiliation with *Poetry*, one of the most influential literary magazines of its time. In Stark's all-black workshop, held in the South Shore Community Center, writers studied Modernist poets and rigorously critiqued one another's work. In Brooks's teenage correspondence with James Weldon Johnson (whose 1922 and 1931 editions of the *Book of American Negro Poetry* would undoubtedly have brought the best of the African-American tradition to the young poet), Johnson had urged her to read Eliot, Pound, and Cummings; she was well-read on her own, and so already familiar with the Modernists. But the intensive group study and conversation in the Stark workshop was galvanizing. They studied *Poetry* magazine (which Brooks continued to support by creating prizes for the magazine over the years) and moved forward in intent and focus with their poems and ambitions. Though Brooks had first published poems when she was a teenager, during this period she began to see publication in serious journals and to win prizes.

Brooks's first collection of poems, *A Street in Bronzeville*, was published by Harper & Brothers in 1945. The poet Paul Engle wrote the book's first review, in the *Chicago Tribune* book section: "The publication of *A Street in*

Bronzeville is an exceptional event in the literary life of Chicago, for it is the first book of a solidly Chicago person." He called her a "young but permanent talent."

The poems of *A Street in Bronzeville* incorporate many aspects of poetic tradition and conversation. Brooks is attuned to the sounds heard and spoken in various spaces on Chicago's South Side. "If you wanted a poem," she wrote in her autobiography, "you only had to look out of a window. There was material always, walking or running, fighting or screaming or singing." She writes of the front and back yards, beauty shops, vacant lots, and bars. Her formal range is most impressive, as she experiments with sonnets, ballads, spirituals, blues, full and off-rhymes. She is nothing short of a technical virtuoso. Her incisive, distilled portraits of individuals taken together give us a collage of a very specific community, in the fashion of Edgar Lee Masters' *Spoon River Anthology* and Jean Toomer's *Cane*. And in that keen and satisfying specificity are universal questions: How do people tend their dreams in the face of day-to-day struggle? How do people constitute community? How do communities respond when their young are sent off to a war full of ironies and contradictions? How do black communities grapple with the problems of materialism, racism, and blind religiosity? Brooks took especially seriously the inner lives of young black women: their hopes, dreams, aspirations, disappointments. How do they make their analytical voices heard in their communities? She continued to explore these themes in her second book, *Annie Allen*.

In the first half of the twentieth century, black writers were still confronted with the pressure, as had Phillis Wheatley, to effectively "prove" their literacy—and, thus, their humanity—through mastery of European forms. Paul Laurence Dunbar, for example, was a soul tormented by many demons, and he lamented the constraints white audiences placed on his work. According to James Weldon Johnson, Dunbar often said, "I've got to write dialect poetry; it's the only way I can get them to listen to me," and toward the end of his brief life he confessed to Johnson, "I have not grown. I am writing the same things I wrote ten years ago, and I am writing them no better." Countee Cullen knew that many saw him as representative and the future of the race and its prime ambassador on the cultural front. So writing expertly within prescribed European forms was a particular, if implicit, pressure on both these relatively successful black poets, Brooks's generational predecessors whom we know she read and studied and who, like her, favored the sonnet. This form suited Dunbar and Cullen and they spread their wings elegantly within it, but they also labored under the expectation that certain rules must be followed in order to assure one's place within the mainstream canon. Brooks, on the other hand, worked with expert subtlety to make the sonnet her own.

In *A Street in Bronzeville*, she concludes with a series of off-rhyme sonnets on black soldiers in World War II, "Gay Chaps at the Bar." Brooks grasped the profound contradictions these soldiers faced, fighting for their country but knowing all along that they would remain second-class citizens—think, for example, of black soldiers who liberated concentration camps being forced to ride in the back cars of military trains upon their return while German prisoners of war rode in the front. Brooks said that the sonnets of "Gay Chaps at the Bar" are off-rhyme because "I felt it was an off-rhyme situation." Within conventional form, Brooks made subtle breaks so that her poetics underscore and enact what she speaks of. In so doing, she makes the form do something unexpected and makes an argument for the absolute rightness and necessity of innovating from within that form to make poetry that speaks power-fully to and out of its black reality.

"The Sundays of Satin-Legs Smith" is the longest poem in *A Street*. Brooks wrote it after Richard Wright evaluated an early version of the book's manuscript for Harpers and observed that most successful volumes of poems had a long centerpiece poem around which the book coalesced. "Sundays" is a tour de force that showcases much Brooksian strength: language that is as "rich" and "elaborate" as Satin-Legs himself but that at the same time displays awareness of its own decoration as well as of the shortcomings of decoration. Satin-Legs is a dandy whose self-image is expressed in his rococo dress and way with the ladies. "He sheds, with his pajamas, shabby days," Brooks writes, and in that shedding and subsequent orna-mentation always leaves behind "his desertedness, his intricate fear, the postponed resentments and the prim pre-cautions." He is in many ways a pitiable character. Brooks shows us the hysterical pitch of his wish for life's beauty ("life must be aromatic. / There must be scent, somehow there must be some.") and yet his wish for and will to beauty is powerful, true, and beautiful unto itself. He loves artifice but also has a "heritage of cabbage and pigtails, / Old intimacy with alleys, garbage pails, / Down in the deep (but always beautiful) South / Where roses blush their blithest (it is said) / And sweet magnolias put Chanel to shame." Brooks also never lets us forget, in the subtlest way, that Satin-Legs' life is set against a backdrop of eco-nomic and racial challenge.

The poem is at its mock-heroic best when Brooks takes the reader through Satin-Legs' closet: "Let us pro-ceed. Let us inspect, together / With his meticulous and serious love, / The innards of this closet." Here she echoes Eliot's Prufrock—"Let us go then, you and I"—another sad character in a similarly ironic "love song" whose love of language and beauty walks a path toward spiritual and emotional drowning. She takes great poetic pleasure in describing Satin-Legs' "wonder-suits in yellow and in wine, / Sarcastic green and zebra-striped cobalt," and yet her empathy forces her to note, without condescension, "People are so in need, in need of help. / People want so much that they do not know." The poem is mock-heroic, lament, and ballad all at once. Brooks goes beneath the masks of thwarted masculinity to show us "men estranged / From music and from wonder and from joy / But far familiar with the guiding awe / Of foodlessness."

In her second book, *Annie Allen*, Brooks invented a form she called the "anniad" for her heroine, a "plain black girl" named Annie Allen whose interior life is richly detailed and deserving its own form; the name of course echoed the *Iliad* and the *Aeneid*. She won the Pulitzer Prize for the book, the first African-American to be so honored. J. Saunders Redding praised *Annie Allen* in *Saturday Review of Literature* but said, "I do not want to see Miss Brooks's fine talents dribble away in the obscure and the too oblique." This note would be sounded intermittently throughout her early career by those who were not responsive to her very particular sense of aesthetics as well as those who expected black literature to speak clearly and directly "to the people" and "their issues." Her response in later years to those pressures would prove dramatic.

Brooks and Blakely's second child, Nora, was born in 1951. Throughout the 1950s Brooks raised her children, reviewed books, worked at her poems, and wrote and published the novel *Maud Martha*. She cast the book as a novel in hopes it would earn her more money than the meager spoils that even a Pulitzer prize–winning poet could expect. *Maud Martha* was well reviewed when it appeared, but it wasn't until the 1980s, with black feminist scholarly interest in teaching and writing about the book, that its extraordinariness became fully appreciated and the book found its place in larger conversations about the African-American novel and formal innovation.

In 1963 she accepted her first teaching job and also published her third collection of poems, *The Bean Eaters*. Many poems in that book were explicitly tied to social issues of the day (though no more so than her poems about World War II and the Bronzeville neighborhood), such as her two poems about Emmett Till, "A Bronzeville Mother Loiters in Mississippi. Meanwhile, a Mississippi Mother Burns Bacon" and "The Last Quatrain of the Ballad of Emmett Till," and "The Chicago *Defender* Sends a Man to Little Rock," which is set in the context of the violent battles for school desegregation. She also further honed the concise short lyric in poems such as "The Bean Eaters," "Old Mary," and her most famous poem, "We Real Cool":

> We real cool. We
> Left school. We
>
> Lurk late. We
> Strike straight. We
>
> Sing sin. We
> Thin gin. We
>
> Jazz June. We
> Die soon.

The poem's brilliance lies in its economy and manipulation of space. By the end, the missing "we" that the poem's pattern has led us to anticipate is a yawning chasm, the absence of the we, these young black boys, from the poem and from the earth once they have frittered their lives away. Brooks read the poem with a swift, whispery "we," moving quickly past the word and using it metronomically to punctuate the rhythm of the poem. The poem's bebop seduces, as the boys at the pool hall are seduced by the finger-popping siren song of the street, which may make you finger-pop but ultimately offers nothing that lasts.

"Bronzeville Woman in a Red Hat" tells a small, explosive story of a white woman who is horrified to see her child kissed by the black maid. Brooks concentrates all the energy and focus of the poem on the single moment in which the white mother witnesses this kiss and experiences:

> Heat at the hairline, heat between the bowels,
> Examining seeming coarse unnatural scene,
> She saw all things except herself serene:
> Child, big black woman, pretty kitchen towels.

This is a scenario Brooks has explored in poems like "A Bronzeville Mother Loiters . . .": the corrosive effects of racism on the children and white women who are a part of its system. She critiques ideologies of domestic order and white femininity that would have white women believe that the pedestals on which they've been placed are desirable and secure. That devastating line, "She saw all things except herself serene" is where Brooks puts the mirror to her character's face and exposes the woman's sense of superiority and order.

Most critics, and Brooks herself, divide her creative life into two parts. The dividing line was 1967, when at the Fisk writers' conference—in the confrontational midst of vibrant young black writers who were envisioning a new social order and the role the arts should play in it—she had a revelation. "It frightens me to realize that if I had died before the age of fifty," she wrote in her autobiography, "I would have died a 'negro' fraction." She soon left the mainstream publishing house Harper and Row and intensified her relationship and affiliation with young black poets such as Haki Madhubuti (formerly Don L. Lee), wearing her hair in what she called a "natural," that most symbolic of hairstyles, the Afro. Further, the style of her work changed discernibly. The tight formal coil of her previous work loosened and the allusions and references were no longer as dense.

Her subject matter did not change—her subjects were still mostly black people who lived in the kitchenette apartments of Bronzeville. Brooks was always clear in her work about who black people were and what it meant to write about them. Her final collection for Harper and Row was *In the Mecca*, published in 1968. Brooks aficionados will notice one major omission from this collection, her great late 1960s epic "In the Mecca." It is only length that prevented its inclusion here. Brooks tried to write this important poem for over thirty years—including a version in prose— after her brief stint working for a charlatan "spiritual adviser" named French who sold love and luck potions door to door in the Mecca apartment building in Chicago. The poem centers on the drama of a child named Pepita, who has gone missing in the warrens of the decrepit building. We meet the building's residents who together form a portrait of a black community along the lines of *A Street in Bronzeville*. But in "In the Mecca" the community is in crisis and has fallen prey to its own problems. The child, who is a poet and the hope of her family and community, is found murdered under the bed of one of the building's residents. The poem ends and so closes the first half of the book in an awful silence that asks, in 1968, what next? The poems included here from *In the Mecca* (from "Boy Breaking Glass" to "The Second Sermon on the Warpland") serve as an answer to that question as the community reconstitutes itself and finds a philosophy ("Conduct your blooming in the noise and whip of the whirlwind") with which to move forward.

After *In the Mecca*, Brooks published only with black presses, from Dudley Randall's Broadside Press to her own The David Company, ending with Madhubuti's Third World Press. She continued to explore form and its challenges in her poems as she asked herself what it meant for her to be "an African poet." The long poem "The Near-Johannesburg Boy," written before the end of apartheid and with its powerful refrain "We shall flail in the Hot Time," concludes without punctuation. Brooks said she did that "because there's no punctuation in that situation." She also coined the term and form "verse journalism" (as she had coined "sonnet-ballad" earlier) for the remarkable piece commissioned by *Ebony* magazine and published in August 1971, "In Montgomery," which explored that seat of the civil rights movement in the words of its residents, after the whirl of that "hot time" was stilled. The poem was recently published in book form with other poems, some never before collected, in the posthumous book of the same name.

Brooks's self-commentary was always pithy and vivid. In an interview conducted by Professor Joanne Gabbin, who created the Furious Flower Poetry Festival at James Madison University to commemorate Brooks's work specifically and African-American poetry in general, Brooks made these assessments: "I am 'an organic' Chicagoan." "The Black experience is any experience that a Black person has." "I want to report; I want to record. I go inside myself, bring out what I feel, put it on paper, look at it, pull out all of the clichés. I will work hard in *that* way." "I don't like the term African American. It is very excluding. I like to think of Blacks as family. . . . As a people, we are not of one accord on what we should be called. Some people say it doesn't matter, 'call me anything.' I think *that* is a pitiful decision."

Brooks titled her collected poems *Blacks*. She continually strove to articulate an unambiguous race pride in a woman's voice that was true to the complex and contradictory poetic details of black people's lives. She was not hyperbolical; she wrote of mighty heroes and those with feet of clay. In her very celebratoriness she practiced a kind of sober love for community. In *In the Mecca*, for example, she described "blackness stern and blunt and beautiful, / organ-rich blackness telling a terrible story." She makes her readers think emotionally and philosophically about what it is to be black and therefore human, to struggle through blackness to struggle against and within one's community. She made public her own struggle for racial self-acceptance in her autobiography, and she was a pioneer in her presentation of the intimate perspectives of young black protagonists whose ideas often ran counter to any expected communal doctrine.

In December 2000, Brooks died at 83. Her loved ones at her bedside said that she died literally pen in hand. On the day of her funeral, Chicago saw a snowstorm wilder and fiercer than any in years. Nonetheless, people came from all over to celebrate that great life, soul, and artistic accomplishment. There was a sense of an era coming to a close. Brooks's work moved with the times, but her early poems remained indelible. In the 1940s her remarkable voice burst on the scene, and she was an acclaimed poet for the entire second half of the twentieth century, taking us from the age of the Harlem Renaissance through twenty years past the Black Arts and Black Power movements. She was a central figure in the equally potent parallel movements in Chicago, the late years of the Chicago renaissance in the early 1940s and then the Chicago Black Arts movement, which in a sense was institutionalized with the Gwendolyn Brooks Center at Chicago State University and the creative writing MFA there (only the second at a predominately black university), which uses writers of Africa and the African Diaspora as its core.

The late jazz-folk singer Oscar Brown, Jr., with whom Brooks worked in community arts in the early 1960s in Chicago, sang a song called "Elegy," which is Brooks's "of DeWitt Williams on his way to Lincoln Cemetery" set to music. The poem invokes the spiritual "Swing Low Sweet Chariot," but as Brown sang it, he invoked no tonal remnant of the original. The poem refuses to "carry me home." Perhaps there is no heaven for DeWitt Williams, no heaven for so many "plain" black boys and girls, those whom Brooks "loved so well" in her poems. The repetition of "sweet" in the line "sweet sweet chariot" resists the full match of the spiritual reference and emphasizes instead the sweet life DeWitt and so many like him loved and which in part took him down: sweet women, sweet wine, "liquid joy." And yet, true sweetness, too, which Brooks knew and understood and respected because she knew and respected the people she wrote about. She wrote truly great poems whose technical achievements are still guiding many poets. The taut strength of her lines, her formal rigor combined with subtle invention, her syntactical originality, all hold up over the years. At the end of all of this work, its sense of intimacy is most striking. She wrote poems about people she loved who lived in a place she loved and knew. Those necessary American songs had not been sung before Gwendolyn Brooks and now they have.

Elizabeth Alexander
2005

FROM **A Street in Bronzeville**

kitchenette building

We are things of dry hours and the involuntary plan,
Grayed in, and gray. "Dream" makes a giddy sound, not
    strong
Like "rent," "feeding a wife," "satisfying a man."

But could a dream send up through onion fumes
Its white and violet, fight with fried potatoes
And yesterday's garbage ripening in the hall,
Flutter, or sing an aria down these rooms

Even if we were willing to let it in,
Had time to warm it, keep it very clean,
Anticipate a message, let it begin?

We wonder. But not well! not for a minute!
Since Number Five is out of the bathroom now,
We think of lukewarm water, hope to get in it.

the mother

Abortions will not let you forget.
You remember the children you got that you did not
    get,
The damp small pulps with a little or with no hair,
The singers and workers that never handled the air.
You will never neglect or beat
Them, or silence or buy with a sweet.
You will never wind up the sucking-thumb
Or scuttle off ghosts that come.
You will never leave them, controlling your luscious
    sigh,
Return for a snack of them, with gobbling mother-eye.

I have heard in the voices of the wind the voices of my
    dim killed children.
I have contracted. I have eased
My dim dears at the breasts they could never suck.
I have said, Sweets, if I sinned, if I seized
Your luck
And your lives from your unfinished reach,
If I stole your births and your names,
Your straight baby tears and your games,
Your stilted or lovely loves, your tumults, your
    marriages, aches, and your deaths,
If I poisoned the beginnings of your breaths,
Believe that even in my deliberateness I was not
    deliberate.
Though why should I whine,
Whine that the crime was other than mine?—

Since anyhow you are dead.
Or rather, or instead,
You were never made.
But that too, I am afraid,
Is faulty: oh, what shall I say, how is the truth to be said?
You were born, you had body, you died.
It is just that you never giggled or planned or cried.

Believe me, I loved you all.
Believe me, I knew you, though faintly, and I loved, I
     loved you
All.

hunchback girl: she thinks of heaven

My Father, it is surely a blue place
And straight. Right. Regular. Where I shall find
No need for scholarly nonchalance or looks
A little to the left or guards upon the
Heart to halt love that runs without crookedness
Along its crooked corridors. My Father,
It is a planned place surely. Out of coils,
Unscrewed, released, no more to be marvelous,
I shall walk straightly through most proper halls
Proper myself, princess of properness.

a song in the front yard

I've stayed in the front yard all my life.
I want a peek at the back
Where it's rough and untended and hungry weed grows.
A girl gets sick of a rose.

I want to go in the back yard now
And maybe down the alley,
To where the charity children play.
I want a good time today.

They do some wonderful things.
They have some wonderful fun.
My mother sneers, but I say it's fine
How they don't have to go in at quarter to nine.
My mother, she tells me that Johnnie Mae
Will grow up to be a bad woman.
That George'll be taken to Jail soon or late
(On account of last winter he sold our back gate.)

But I say it's fine. Honest, I do.
And I'd like to be a bad woman, too,
And wear the brave stockings of night-black lace
And strut down the streets with paint on my face.

the ballad of chocolate Mabbie

It was Mabbie without the grammar school gates.
And Mabbie was all of seven.
And Mabbie was cut from a chocolate bar.
And Mabbie thought life was heaven.

The grammar school gates were the pearly gates,
For Willie Boone went to school.
When she sat by him in history class
Was only her eyes were cool.

It was Mabbie without the grammar school gates
Waiting for Willie Boone.
Half hour after the closing bell!
He would surely be coming soon.

Oh, warm is the waiting for joys, my dears!
And it cannot be too long.
Oh, pity the little poor chocolate lips
That carry the bubble of song!

Out came the saucily bold Willie Boone.
It was woe for our Mabbie now.
He wore like a jewel a lemon-hued lynx
With sand-waves loving her brow.

It was Mabbie alone by the grammar school gates.
Yet chocolate companions had she:
Mabbie on Mabbie with hush in the heart.
Mabbie on Mabbie to be.

the preacher: ruminates behind the sermon

I think it must be lonely to be God.
Nobody loves a master. No. Despite
The bright hosannas, bright dear-Lords, and bright
Determined reverence of Sunday eyes.

Picture Jehovah striding through the hall
Of His importance, creatures running out
From servant-corners to acclaim, to shout
Appreciation of His merit's glare.

But who walks with Him?—dares to take His arm,
To slap Him on the shoulder, tweak His ear,
Buy Him a Coca-Cola or a beer,
Pooh-pooh His politics, call Him a fool?

Perhaps—who knows?—He tires of looking down.
Those eyes are never lifted. Never straight.
Perhaps sometimes He tires of being great
In solitude. Without a hand to hold.

Sadie and Maud

Maud went to college.
Sadie stayed at home.
Sadie scraped life
With a fine-tooth comb.

She didn't leave a tangle in.
Her comb found every strand.
Sadie was one of the livingest chits
In all the land.

Sadie bore two babies
Under her maiden name.
Maud and Ma and Papa
Nearly died of shame.
Every one but Sadie
Nearly died of shame.

When Sadie said her last so-long
Her girls struck out from home.
(Sadie had left as heritage
Her fine-tooth comb.)

Maud, who went to college,
Is a thin brown mouse.
She is living all alone
In this old house.

when you have forgotten Sunday: the love story

——And when you have forgotten the bright bedclothes
    on a Wednesday and a Saturday,
And most especially when you have forgotten Sunday—
When you have forgotten Sunday halves in bed,
Or me sitting on the front-room radiator in the limping
    afternoon

Looking off down the long street
To nowhere,
Hugged by my plain old wrapper of no-expectation
And nothing-I-have-to-do and I'm-happy-why?
And if-Monday-never-had-to-come—
When you have forgotten that, I say,
And how you swore, if somebody beeped the bell,
And how my heart played hopscotch if the telephone
    rang;
And how we finally went in to Sunday dinner,
That is to say, went across the front room floor to the
    ink-spotted table in the southwest corner
To Sunday dinner, which was always chicken and
    noodles
Or chicken and rice
And salad and rye bread and tea
And chocolate chip cookies—
I say, when you have forgotten that,
When you have forgotten my little presentiment
That the war would be over before they got to you;
And how we finally undressed and whipped out the light
    and flowed into bed,
And lay loose-limbed for a moment in the week-end
Bright bedclothes,
Then gently folded into each other—
When you have, I say, forgotten all that,
Then you may tell,
Then I may believe
You have forgotten me well.

He was born in Alabama.
He was bred in Illinois.
He was nothing but a
Plain black boy.

Swing low swing low sweet sweet chariot.
Nothing but a plain black boy.

Drive him past the Pool Hall.
Drive him past the Show.
Blind within his casket,
But maybe he will know.

Down through Forty-seventh Street:
Underneath the L,
And—Northwest Corner, Prairie,
That he loved so well.

Don't forget the Dance Halls—
Warwick and Savoy,
Where he picked his women, where
He drank his liquid joy.

Born in Alabama.
Bred in Illinois.
He was nothing but a
Plain black boy.

Swing low swing low sweet sweet chariot.
Nothing but a plain black boy.

the vacant lot

Mrs. Coley's three-flat brick
Isn't here any more.
All done with seeing her fat little form
Burst out of the basement door;
And with seeing her African son-in-law
(Rightful heir to the throne)
With his great white strong cold squares of teeth
And his little eyes of stone;
And with seeing the squat fat daughter
Letting in the men
When majesty has gone for the day—
And letting them out again.

The Sundays of Satin-Legs Smith

Inamoratas, with an approbation,
Bestowed his title. Blessed his inclination.

He wakes, unwinds, elaborately: a cat
Tawny, reluctant, royal. He is fat
And fine this morning. Definite. Reimbursed.

He waits a moment, he designs his reign,
That no performance may be plain or vain.
Then rises in a clear delirium.

He sheds, with his pajamas, shabby days.
And his desertedness, his intricate fear, the
Postponed resentments and the prim precautions.

Now, at his bath, would you deny him lavender
Or take away the power of his pine?
What smelly substitute, heady as wine,
Would you provide? life must be aromatic.
There must be scent, somehow there must be some.
Would you have flowers in his life? suggest
Asters? a Really Good geranium?
A white carnation? would you prescribe a Show
With the cold lilies, formal chrysanthemum
Magnificence, poinsettias, and emphatic
Red of prize roses? might his happiest
Alternative (you muse) be, after all,
A bit of gentle garden in the best
Of taste and straight tradition? Maybe so.
But you forget, or did you ever know,
His heritage of cabbage and pigtails,
Old intimacy with alleys, garbage pails,
Down in the deep (but always beautiful) South
Where roses blush their blithest (it is said)
And sweet magnolias put Chanel to shame.

No! He has not a flower to his name.
Except a feather one, for his lapel.
Apart from that, if he should think of flowers
It is in terms of dandelions or death.
Ah, there is little hope. You might as well—
Unless you care to set the world a-boil

And do a lot of equalizing things,
Remove a little ermine, say, from kings,
Shake hands with paupers and appoint them men,
For instance—certainly you might as well
Leave him his lotion, lavender and oil.

Let us proceed. Let us inspect, together
With his meticulous and serious love,
The innards of this closet. Which is a vault
Whose glory is not diamonds, not pearls,
Not silver plate with just enough dull shine.
But wonder-suits in yellow and in wine,
Sarcastic green and zebra-striped cobalt.
All drapes. With shoulder padding that is wide
And cocky and determined as his pride;
Ballooning pants that taper off to ends
Scheduled to choke precisely.
                                        Here are hats
Like bright umbrellas; and hysterical ties
Like narrow banners for some gathering war.

People are so in need, in need of help.
People want so much that they do not know.

Below the tinkling trade of little coins
The gold impulse not possible to show
Or spend. Promise piled over and betrayed.

These kneaded limbs receive the kiss of silk.
Then they receive the brave and beautiful
Embrace of some of that equivocal wool.

He looks into his mirror, loves himself—
The neat curve here; the angularity
That is appropriate at just its place;
The technique of a variegated grace.

Here is all his sculpture and his art
And all his architectural design.
Perhaps you would prefer to this a fine
Value of marble, complicated stone.
Would have him think with horror of baroque,
Rococo. You forget and you forget.

He dances down the hotel steps that keep
Remnants of last night's high life and distress.
As spat-out purchased kisses and spilled beer.
He swallows sunshine with a secret yelp.
Passes to coffee and a roll or two.
Has breakfasted.

               Out. Sounds about him smear,
Become a unit. He hears and does not hear
The alarm clock meddling in somebody's sleep;
Children's governed Sunday happiness;
The dry tone of a plane; a woman's oath;
Consumption's spiritless expectoration;
An indignant robin's resolute donation
Pinching a track through apathy and din;
Restaurant vendors weeping; and the L
That comes on like a slightly horrible thought.

Pictures, too, as usual, are blurred.
He sees and does not see the broken windows

Hiding their shame with newsprint; little girl
With ribbons decking wornness, little boy
Wearing the trousers with the decentest patch,
To honor Sunday; women on their way
From "service," temperate holiness arranged
Ably on asking faces; men estranged
From music and from wonder and from joy
But far familiar with the guiding awe
Of foodlessness.

         He loiters.

                Restaurant vendors
Weep, or out of them rolls a restless glee.
The Lonesome Blues, the Long-lost Blues, I Want A
Big Fat Mama. Down these sore avenues
Comes no Saint-Saëns, no piquant elusive Grieg,
And not Tschaikovsky's wayward eloquence
And not the shapely tender drift of Brahms.
But could he love them? Since a man must bring
To music what his mother spanked him for
When he was two: bits of forgotten hate,
Devotion: whether or not his mattress hurts:
The little dream his father humored: the thing
His sister did for money: what he ate
For breakfast—and for dinner twenty years
Ago last autumn: all his skipped desserts.

The pasts of his ancestors lean against
Him. Crowd him. Fog out his identity.
Hundreds of hungers mingle with his own,
Hundreds of voices advise so dexterously
He quite considers his reactions his,

Judges he walks most powerfully alone,
That everything is—simply what it is.

But movie-time approaches, time to boo
The hero's kiss, and boo the heroine
Whose ivory and yellow it is sin
For his eye to eat of. The Mickey Mouse,
However, is for everyone in the house.

Squires his lady to dinner at Joe's Eats.
His lady alters as to leg and eye,
Thickness and height, such minor points as these,
From Sunday to Sunday. But no matter what
Her name or body positively she's
In Queen Lace stockings with ambitious heels
That strain to kiss the calves, and vivid shoes
Frontless and backless, Chinese fingernails,
Earrings, three layers of lipstick, intense hat
Dripping with the most voluble of veils.
Her affable extremes are like sweet bombs
About him, whom no middle grace or good
Could gratify. He had no education
In quiet arts of compromise. He would
Not understand your counsels on control, nor
Thank you for your late trouble.

                              At Joe's Eats
You get your fish or chicken on meat platters.
With coleslaw, macaroni, candied sweets,
Coffee and apple pie. You go out full.
(The end is—isn't it?—all that really matters.)

And even and intrepid come
The tender boots of night to home.

Her body is like new brown bread
Under the Woolworth mignonette.
Her body is a honey bowl
Whose waiting honey is deep and hot.
Her body is like summer earth,
Receptive, soft, and absolute . . .

Negro Hero

to suggest Dorie Miller

I had to kick their law into their teeth in order to save
    them.
However I have heard that sometimes you have to deal
Devilishly with drowning men in order to swim them to
    shore.
Or they will haul themselves and you to the trash and
    the fish beneath.
(When I think of this, I do not worry about a few
Chipped teeth.)

It is good I gave glory, it is good I put gold on their
    name.
Or there would have been spikes in the afterward hands.
But let us speak only of my success and the pictures in
    the Caucasian dailies
As well as the Negro weeklies. For I am a gem.

(They are not concerned that it was hardly The Enemy
        my fight was against
But them.)

It was a tall time. And of course my blood was
Boiling about in my head and straining and howling and
        singing me on.
Of course I was rolled on wheels of my boy itch to get at
        the gun.
Of course all the delicate rehearsal shots of my child-
        hood massed in mirage before me.
Of course I was child
And my first swallow of the liquor of battle bleeding
        black air dying and demon noise
Made me wild.

It was kinder than that, though, and I showed like a
        banner my kindness.
I loved. And a man will guard when he loves.
Their white-gowned democracy was my fair lady.
With her knife lying cold, straight, in the softness of her
        sweet-flowing sleeve.
But for the sake of the dear smiling mouth and the
        stuttered promise I toyed with my life.
I threw back!—I would not remember
Entirely the knife.

Still—am I good enough to die for them, is my blood
        bright enough to be spilled,
Was my constant back-question—are they clear
On this? Or do I intrude even now?

Am I clean enough to kill for them, do they wish me to kill
For them or is my place while death licks his lips and
     strides to them
In the galley still?

(In a southern city a white man said
Indeed, I'd rather be dead;
Indeed, I'd rather be shot in the head
Or ridden to waste on the back of a flood
Than saved by the drop of a black man's blood.)

Naturally, the important thing is, I helped to save them,
     them and a part of their democracy.
Even if I had to kick their law into their teeth in order
     to do that for them.
And I am feeling well and settled in myself because I
     believe it was a good job,
Despite this possible horror: that they might prefer the
Preservation of their law in all its sick dignity and their
     knives
To the continuation of their creed
And their lives.

Ballad of Pearl May Lee

Then off they took you, off to the jail,
A hundred hooting after.
And you should have heard me at my house.
I cut my lungs with my laughter,

Laughter,
Laughter.
I cut my lungs with my laughter.

They dragged you into a dusty cell.
And a rat was in the corner.
And what was I doing? Laughing still.
Though never was a poor gal lorner,
    Lorner,
    Lorner.
Though never was a poor gal lorner.

The sheriff, he peeped in through the bars,
And (the red old thing) he told you,
"You son of a bitch, you're going to hell!"
'Cause you wanted white arms to enfold you,
    Enfold you,
    Enfold you.
'Cause you wanted white arms to enfold you.

But you paid for your white arms, Sammy boy,
And you didn't pay with money.
You paid with your hide and my heart, Sammy boy,
For your taste of pink and white honey,
    Honey,
    Honey.
For your taste of pink and white honey.

Oh, dig me out of my don't-despair.
Pull me out of my poor-me.
Get me a garment of red to wear.

You had it coming surely,
   Surely,
   Surely,
You had it coming surely.

At school, your girls were the bright little girls.
You couldn't abide dark meat.
Yellow was for to look at,
Black for the famished to eat.
Yellow was for to look at,
Black for the famished to eat.

You grew up with bright skins on the brain,
And me in your black folks bed.
Often and often you cut me cold,
And often I wished you dead.
Often and often you cut me cold.
Often I wished you dead.

Then a white girl passed you by one day,
And, the vixen, she gave you the wink.
And your stomach got sick and your legs liquefied.
And you thought till you couldn't think.
   You thought,
   You thought,
You thought till you couldn't think.

I fancy you out on the fringe of town,
The moon an owl's eye minding;
The sweet and thick of the cricket-belled dark,
The fire within you winding . . . .

Winding,
Winding . . . .
The fire within you winding.

Say, she was white like milk, though, wasn't she?
And her breasts were cups of cream.
In the back of her Buick you drank your fill.
Then she roused you out of your dream.
In the back of her Buick you drank your fill.
Then she roused you out of your dream.

"You raped me, nigger," she softly said.
(The shame was threading through.)
"You raped me, nigger, and what the hell
Do you think I'm going to do?
    What the hell,
    What the hell
Do you think I'm going to do?

"I'll tell every white man in this town.
I'll tell them all of my sorrow.
You got my body tonight, nigger boy.
I'll get your body tomorrow.
    Tomorrow.
    Tomorrow.
I'll get your body tomorrow."

And my glory but Sammy she did! She did!
And they stole you out of the jail.
They wrapped you around a cottonwood tree.
And they laughed when they heard you wail.

Laughed,
Laughed.
They laughed when they heard you wail.

And I was laughing, down at my house.
Laughing fit to kill.
You got what you wanted for dinner,
But brother you paid the bill.
　　Brother,
　　Brother,
Brother you paid the bill.

You paid for your dinner, Sammy boy,
And you didn't pay with money.
You paid with your hide and my heart, Sammy boy,
For your taste of pink and white honey,
　　Honey,
　　Honey.
For your taste of pink and white honey.

Oh, dig me out of my don't-despair.
Oh, pull me out of my poor-me.
Oh, get me a garment of red to wear.
You had it coming surely.
　　Surely.
　　Surely.
You had it coming surely.

souvenir for Staff Sergeant Raymond Brooks and every other soldier

gay chaps at the bar

> . . . and guys I knew in the States, young officers, return
> from the front crying and trembling. Gay chaps at the
> bar in Los Angeles, Chicago, New York. . . .
>
> LIEUTENANT WILLIAM COUCH
> in the South Pacific

We knew how to order. Just the dash
Necessary. The length of gaiety in good taste.
Whether the raillery should be slightly iced
And given green, or served up hot and lush.
And we knew beautifully how to give to women
The summer spread, the tropics, of our love.
When to persist, or hold a hunger off.
Knew white speech. How to make a look an omen.
But nothing ever taught us to be islands.
And smart, athletic language for this hour
Was not in the curriculum. No stout
Lesson showed how to chat with death. We brought
No brass fortissimo, among our talents,
To holler down the lions in this air.

still do I keep my look, my identity . . .

Each body has its art, its precious prescribed
Pose, that even in passion's droll contortions, waltzes,
Or push of pain—or when a grief has stabbed,

Or hatred hacked—is its, and nothing else's.
Each body has its pose. No other stock
That is irrevocable, perpetual
And its to keep. In castle or in shack.
With rags or robes. Through good, nothing, or ill.
And even in death a body, like no other
On any hill or plain or crawling cot
Or gentle for the lilyless hasty pall
(Having twisted, gagged, and then sweet-ceased bother),
Shows the old personal art, the look. Shows what
It showed at baseball. What it showed in school.

my dreams, my works, must wait till after hell

I hold my honey and I store my bread
In little jars and cabinets of my will.
I label clearly, and each latch and lid
I bid, Be firm till I return from hell.
I am very hungry. I am incomplete.
And none can tell when I may dine again.
No man can give me any word but Wait,
The puny light. I keep eyes pointed in;
Hoping that, when the devil days of my hurt
Drag out to their last dregs and I resume
On such legs as are left me, in such heart
As I can manage, remember to go home,
My taste will not have turned insensitive
To honey and bread old purity could love.

looking

You have no word for soldiers to enjoy
The feel of, as an apple, and to chew
With masculine satisfaction. Not "good-by!"
"Come back!" or "careful!" Look, and let him go.
"Good-by!" is brutal, and "come back!" the raw
Insistence of an idle desperation
Since could he favor he would favor now.
He will be "careful!" if he has permission.
Looking is better. At the dissolution
Grab greatly with the eye, crush in a steel
Of study—Even that is vain. Expression,
The touch or look or word, will little avail,
The brawniest will not beat back the storm
Nor the heaviest haul your little boy from harm.

mentors

For I am rightful fellow of their band.
My best allegiances are to the dead.
I swear to keep the dead upon my mind,
Disdain for all time to be overglad.
Among spring flowers, under summer trees,
By chilling autumn waters, in the frosts
Of supercilious winter—all my days
I'll have as mentors those reproving ghosts.
And at that cry, at that remotest whisper,
I'll stop my casual business. Leave the banquet.
Or leave the ball—reluctant to unclasp her

Who may be fragrant as the flower she wears,
Make gallant bows and dim excuses, then quit
Light for the midnight that is mine and theirs.

the white troops had their orders
but the Negroes looked like men

They had supposed their formula was fixed.
They had obeyed instructions to devise
A type of cold, a type of hooded gaze.
But when the Negroes came they were perplexed.
These Negroes looked like men. Besides, it taxed
Time and the temper to remember those
Congenital iniquities that cause
Disfavor of the darkness. Such as boxed
Their feelings properly, complete to tags—
A box for dark men and a box for Other—
Would often find the contents had been scrambled.
Or even switched. Who really gave two figs?
Neither the earth nor heaven ever trembled.
And there was nothing startling in the weather.

love note
I: surely

Surely you stay my certain own, you stay
My you. All honest, lofty as a cloud.
Surely I could come now and find you high,
As mine as you ever were; should not be awed.

Surely your word would pop as insolent
As always: "Why, of course I love you, dear."
Your gaze, surely, ungauzed as I could want.
Your touches, that never were careful, what they were.
Surely—But I am very off from that.
From surely. From indeed. From the decent arrow
That was my clean naïveté and my faith.
This morning men deliver wounds and death.
They will deliver death and wounds tomorrow.
And I doubt all. You. Or a violet.

    the progress

And still we wear our uniforms, follow
The cracked cry of the bugles, comb and brush
Our pride and prejudice, doctor the sallow
Initial ardor, wish to keep it fresh.
Still we applaud the President's voice and face.
Still we remark on patriotism, sing,
Salute the flag, thrill heavily, rejoice
For death of men who too saluted, sang.
But inward grows a soberness, an awe,
A fear, a deepening hollow through the cold.
For even if we come out standing up
How shall we smile, congratulate: and how
Settle in chairs? Listen, listen. The step
Of iron feet again. And again   wild.

Notes from the Childhood and the Girlhood

1   *the birth in a narrow room*

Weeps out of western country something new.
Blurred and stupendous. Wanted and unplanned.
  Winks. Twines, and weakly winks
Upon the milk-glass fruit bowl, iron pot,
The bashful china child tipping forever
Yellow apron and spilling pretty cherries.

Now, weeks and years will go before she thinks
"How pinchy is my room! how can I breathe!
I am not anything and I have got
Not anything, or anything to do!"—
But prances nevertheless with gods and fairies
Blithely about the pump and then beneath
The elms and grapevines, then in darling endeavor
By privy foyer, where the screenings stand
And where the bugs buzz by in private cars
Across old peach cans and old jelly jars.

Maxie Allen always taught her
Stipendiary little daughter
To thank her Lord and lucky star
For eye that let her see so far,
For throat enabling her to eat
Her Quaker Oats and Cream-of-Wheat,
For tongue to tantrum for the penny,
For ear to hear the haven't-any,
For arm to toss, for leg to chance,
For heart to hanker for romance.

Sweet Annie tried to teach her mother
There was somewhat of something other.
And whether it was veils and God
And whistling ghosts to go unshod
Across the broad and bitter sod,
Or fleet love stopping at her foot
And giving her its never-root
To put into her pocket-book,
Or just a deep and human look,
She did not know; but tried to tell.

Her mother thought at her full well,
In inner voice not like a bell
(Which though not social has a ring
Akin to wrought bedevilling)
But like an oceanic thing:
    What do you guess I am?
    You've lots of jacks and strawberry jam.

And you don't have to go to bed, I remark,
With two dill pickles in the dark,
Nor prop what hardly calls you honey
And gives you only a little money.

3   *the parents: people like our marriage*
            Maxie and Andrew

Clogged and soft and sloppy eyes
Have lost the light that bites or terrifies.

There are no swans and swallows any more.
The people settled for chicken and shut the door.

But one by one
They got things done:
Watch for porches as you pass
And prim low fencing pinching in the grass.

Pleasant custards sit behind
The white Venetian blind.

4   *Sunday chicken*

Chicken, she chided early, should not wait
Under the cranberries in after-sermon state.
Who had been beaking about the yard of late.

Elite among the speckle-gray, wild white
On blundering mosaic in the night.
Or lovely baffle-brown. It was not right.

You could not hate the cannibal they wrote
Of, with the nostril bone-thrust, who could dote
On boiled or roasted fellow thigh and throat.

Nor hate the handsome tiger, call him devil
To man-feast, manifesting Sunday evil.

5   *old relative*

After the baths and bowel-work, he was dead.
Pillows no longer mattered, and getting fed
And anything that anybody said.

Whatever was his he never more strictly had,
Lying in long hesitation. Good or bad,
Hypothesis, traditional and fad.

She went in there to muse on being rid
Of relative beneath the coffin lid.
No one was by. She stuck her tongue out; slid.

Since for a week she must not play "Charmaine"
Or "Honey Bunch," or "Singing in the Rain."

What was not pleasant was the hush that coughed
When the Negro clown came on the stage and doffed
His broken hat. The hush, first. Then the soft

Concatenation of delight and lift,
And loud. The decked dismissal of his gift,
The sugared hoot and hauteur. Then, the rift

Where is magnificent, heirloom, and deft
Leer at a Negro to the right, or left—
So joined to personal bleach, and so bereft:

Finding if that is locked, is bowed, or proud.
And what that is at all, spotting the crowd.

7   *the ballad of late Annie*

Late Annie in her bower lay,
Though sun was up and spinning.
The blush-brown shoulder was so bare,
Blush-brown lip was winning.

Out then shrieked the mother-dear,
"Be I to fetch and carry?
Get a broom to whish the doors
Or get a man to marry."

"Men there were and men there be
But never men so many

Chief enough to marry me,"
Thought the proud late Annie.

"Whom I raise my shades before
Must be gist and lacquer.
With melted opals for my milk,
Pearl-leaf for my cracker."

8   *throwing out the flowers*

The duck fats rot in the roasting pan,
And it's over and over and all,
The fine fraught smiles, and spites that began
Before it was over and all.

The Thanksgiving praying's away with the silk.
It's over and over and all.
The broccoli, yams and the bead-buttermilk
Are dead with the hail in the hall,
    All
Are dead with the hail in the hall.

The three yellow 'mums and the one white 'mum
Bear to such brusque burial
With pity for little encomium
Since it's over and over and all.

Forgotten and stinking they stick in the can,
And the vase breath's better and all, and all.
And so for the end of our life to a man,
Just over, just over and all.

"Do not be afraid of no,
Who has so far so very far to go":

New caution to occur
To one whose inner scream set her to cede, for softer
     lapping and smooth fur!

Whose esoteric need
Was merely to avoid the nettle, to not-bleed.

Stupid, like a street
That beats into a dead end and dies there, with nothing
     left to reprimand or meet.

And like a candle fixed
Against dismay and countershine of mixed

Wild moon and sun. And like
A flying furniture, or bird with lattice wing; or gaunt
     thing, a-stammer down a nightmare neon peopled
     with condor, hawk and shrike.

To say yes is to die
A lot or a little. The dead wear capably their wry

Enameled emblems. They smell.
But that and that they do not altogether yell is all that
     we know well.

It is brave to be involved,
To be not fearful to be unresolved.

Her new wish was to smile
When answers took no airships, walked a while.

10   *"pygmies are pygmies still, though*
      percht on Alps"

                    —EDWARD YOUNG

But can see better there, and laughing there
Pity the giants wallowing on the plain.
Giants who bleat and chafe in their small grass,
Seldom to spread the palm; to spit; come clean.

Pygmies expand in cold impossible air,
Cry fie on giantshine, poor glory which
Pounds breast-bone punily, screeches, and has
Reached no Alps: or, knows no Alps to reach.

11   *my own sweet good*

"Not needing, really, my own sweet good,
To dimple you every day,
For knowing you roam like a gold half-god
And your golden promise was gay.

"Somewhere, you put on your overcoat,
And the others mind what you say
Ill-knowing your route rides to me, roundabout.
For promise so golden and gay.

"Somewhere, you lattice your berries with bran,
Readying for riding my way.
You kiss all the great-lipped girls that you can.
If only they knew that it's little today
And nothing tomorrow to take or to pay,
For sake of a promise so golden, gay,
For promise so golden and gay."

The Anniad

The Anniad

Think of sweet and chocolate,
Left to folly or to fate,
Whom the higher gods forgot,
Whom the lower gods berate;
Physical and underfed
Fancying on the featherbed
What was never and is not.

What is ever and is not.
Pretty tatters blue and red,
Buxom berries beyond rot,
Western clouds and quarter-stars,

Fairy-sweet of old guitars
Littering the little head
Light upon the featherbed.

Think of ripe and rompabout,
All her harvest buttoned in,
All her ornaments untried;
Waiting for the paladin
Prosperous and ocean-eyed
Who shall rub her secrets out
And behold the hinted bride.

Watching for the paladin
Which no woman ever had,
Paradisaical and sad
With a dimple in his chin
And the mountains in the mind;
Ruralist and rather bad,
Cosmopolitan and kind.

Think of thaumaturgic lass
Looking in her looking-glass
At the unembroidered brown;
Printing bastard roses there;
Then emotionally aware
Of the black and boisterous hair,
Taming all that anger down.

And a man of tan engages
For the springtime of her pride,
Eats the green by easy stages,

Nibbles at the root beneath
With intimidating teeth.
But no ravishment enrages.
No dominion is defied.

Narrow master master-calls;
And the godhead glitters now
Cavalierly on his brow.
What a hot theopathy
Roisters through her, gnaws the walls,
And consumes her where she falls
In her gilt humility.

How he postures at his height;
Unfamiliar, to be sure,
With celestial furniture.
Contemplating by cloud-light
His bejewelled diadem;
As for jewels, counting them,
Trying if the pomp be pure.

In the beam his track diffuses
Down her dusted demi-gloom
Like a nun of crimson ruses
She advances. Sovereign
Leaves the heaven she put him in
For the path his pocket chooses;
Leads her to a lowly room.

Which she makes a chapel of.
Where she genuflects to love.

All the prayerbooks in her eyes
Open soft as sacrifice
Or the dolour of a dove.
Tender candles ray by ray
Warm and gratify the gray.

Silver flowers fill the eves
Of the metamorphosis.
And her set excess believes
Incorruptibly that no
Silver has to gape or go,
Deviate to underglow,
Sicken off to hit-or-miss.

Doomer, though, crescendo-comes
Prophesying hecatombs.
Surrealist and cynical.
Garrulous and guttural.
Spits upon the silver leaves.
Denigrates the dainty eves
Dear dexterity achieves.

Names him. Tames him. Takes him off,
Throws to columns row on row.
Where he makes the rifles cough,
Stutter. Where the reveille
Is staccato majesty.
Then to marches. Then to know
The hunched hells across the sea.

Vaunting hands are now devoid.
Hieroglyphics of her eyes
Blink upon a paradise
Paralyzed and paranoid.
But idea and body too
Clamor "Skirmishes can do.
Then he will come back to you."

Less than ruggedly he kindles
Pallors into broken fire.
Hies him home, the bumps and brindles
Of his rummage of desire
Tosses to her lap entire.
Hearing still such eerie stutter.
Caring not if candles gutter.

Tan man twitches: for for long
Life was little as a sand,
Little as an inch of song,
Little as the aching hand
That would fashion mountains, such
Little as a drop from grand
When a heart decides "Too much!"—

Yet there was a drama, drought
Scarleted about the brim
Not with blood alone for him,
Flood, with blossom in between
Retch and wheeling and cold shout,
Suffocation, with a green
Moist sweet breath for mezzanine.

Hometown hums with stoppages.
Now the doughty meanings die
As costumery from streets.
And this white and greater chess
Baffles tan man. Gone the heats
That observe the funny fly
Till the stickum stops the cry.

With his helmet's final doff
Soldier lifts his power off.
Soldier bare and chilly then
Wants his power back again.
No confection languider
Before quick-feast quick-famish Men
Than the candy crowns-that-were.

Hunts a further fervor now.
Shudders for his impotence.
Chases root and vehemence,
Chases stilts and straps to vie
With recession of the sky.
Stiffens: yellows: wonders how
Woman fits for recompense.

Not that woman! (Not that room!
Not that dusted demi-gloom!)
Nothing limpid, nothing meek.
But a gorgeous and gold shriek
With her tongue tucked in her cheek,
Hissing gauzes in her gaze,
Coiling oil upon her ways.

Gets a maple banshee. Gets
A sleek slit-eyed gypsy moan.
Oh those violent vinaigrettes!
Oh bad honey that can hone
Oilily the bluntest stone!
Oh mad bacchanalian lass
That his random passion has!

Think of sweet and chocolate
Minus passing-magistrate,
Minus passing-lofty light,
Minus passing-stars for night,
Sirocco wafts and tra la la,
Minus symbol, cinema
Mirages, all things suave and bright.

Seeks for solaces in snow
In the crusted wintertime.
Icy jewels glint and glow.
Half-blue shadows slanting grow
Over blue and silver rime.
And the crunching in the crust
Chills her nicely, as it must.

Seeks for solaces in green
In the green and fluting spring.
Bubbles apple-green, shrill wine,
Hyacinthine devils sing
In the upper air, unseen
Pucks and cupids make a fine
Fume of fondness and sunshine.

Runs to summer gourmet fare.
Heavy and inert the heat,
Braided round by ropes of scent
With a hypnotist intent.
Think of chocolate and sweet
Wanting richly not to care
That summer hoots at solitaire.

Runs to parks. November leaves
All gone papery and brown
Poise upon the queasy stalks
And perturb the respectable walks.
Glances grayly and perceives
This November her true town:
All's a falling falling down.

Spins, and stretches out to friends.
Cries "I am bedecked with love!"
Cries "I am philanthropist!
Take such rubies as ye list.
Suit to any bonny ends.
Sheathe, expose: but never shove.
Prune, curb, mute: but put above."

Sends down flirting bijouterie.
"Come, oh populace, to me!"
It winks only, and in that light
Are the copies of all her bright
Copies. Glass begets glass. No
Populace goes as they go
Who can need it but at night.

Twists to Plato, Aeschylus,
Seneca and Mimnermus,
Pliny, Dionysius. . . .
Who remove from remarkable hosts
Of agonized and friendly ghosts,
Lean and laugh at one who looks
To find kisses pressed in books.

Tests forbidden taffeta.
Meteors encircle her.
Little lady who lost her twill,
Little lady who lost her fur
Shivers in her thin hurrah,
Pirouettes to pleasant shrill
Appoggiatura with a skill.

But the culprit magics fade.
Stoical the retrograde.
And no music plays at all
In the inner, hasty hall
Which compulsion cut from shade.—
Frees her lover. Drops her hands.
Shorn and taciturn she stands.

Petals at her breast and knee. . . .
"Then incline to children-dear!
Pull the halt magnificence near,
Sniff the perfumes, ribbonize
Gay bouquet most satinly;
Hoard it, for a planned surprise
When the desert terrifies."

Perfumes fly before the gust,
Colors shrivel in the dust,
And the petal velvet shies,
When the desert terrifies:
Howls, revolves, and countercharms:
Shakes its great and gritty arms:
And perplexes with odd eyes.

Hence from scenic bacchanal,
Preshrunk and droll prodigal!
Smallness that you had to spend,
Spent. Wench, whiskey and tail-end
Of your overseas disease
Rot and rout you by degrees.
—Close your fables and fatigues;

Kill that fanged flamingo foam
And the fictive gold that mocks;
Shut your rhetorics in a box;
Pack compunction and go home.
Skeleton, settle, down in bed.
Slide a bone beneath Her head,
Kiss Her eyes so rash and red.

Pursing lips for new good-byeing
Now she folds his rust and cough
In the pity old and staunch.
She remarks his feathers off;
Feathers for such tipsy flying
As this scarcely may re-launch
That is dolesome and is dying.

He leaves bouncy sprouts to store
Caramel dolls a little while,
Then forget him, larger doll
Who would hardly ever loll,
Who would hardly ever smile,
Or bring dill pickles, or core
Fruit, or put salve on a sore.

Leaves his mistress to dismiss
Memories of his kick and kiss,
Grant her lips another smear,
Adjust the posies at her ear,
Quaff an extra pint of beer,
Cross her legs upon the stool,
Slit her eyes and find her fool.

Leaves his devotee to bear
Weight of passing by his chair
And his tavern. Telephone
Hoists her stomach to the air.
Who is starch or who is stone
Washes coffee-cups and hair,
Sweeps, determines what to wear.

In the indignant dark there ride
Roughnesses and spiny things
On infallible hundred heels.
And a bodiless bee stings.
Cyclone concentration reels.
Harried sods dilate, divide,
Suck her sorrowfully inside.

Think of tweaked and twenty-four.
Fuchsias gone or gripped or gray,
All hay-colored that was green.
Soft aesthetic looted, lean.
Crouching low, behind a screen,
Pock-marked eye-light, and the sore
Eaglets of old pride and prey.

Think of almost thoroughly
Derelict and dim and done.
Stroking swallows from the sweat.
Fingering faint violet.
Hugging old and Sunday sun.
Kissing in her kitchenette
The minuets of memory.

Appendix to The Anniad

leaves from a loose-leaf war diary
1
(*"thousands—killed in action"*)

You need the untranslatable ice to watch.
You need to loiter a little among the vague
Hushes, the clever evasions of the vagueness
Above the healthy energy of decay.
You need the untranslatable ice to watch,
The purple and black to smell.

Before your horror can be sweet.
Or proper.
Before your grief is other than discreet.

The intellectual damn
Will nurse your half-hurt. Quickly you are well.

But weary. How you yawn, have yet to see
Why nothing exhausts you like this sympathy.

2

The Certainty we two shall meet by God
In a wide Parlor, underneath a Light
Of lights, come Sometime, is no ointment now.
Because we two are worshipers of life,
Being young, being masters of the long-legged stride,
Gypsy arm-swing. We never did learn how
To find white in the Bible. We want nights
Of vague adventure, lips lax wet and warm,
Bees in the stomach, sweat across the brow. Now.

3 *the sonnet-ballad*

Oh mother, mother, where is happiness?
They took my lover's tallness off to war,
Left me lamenting. Now I cannot guess
What I can use an empty heart-cup for.
He won't be coming back here any more.
Some day the war will end, but, oh, I knew
When he went walking grandly out that door
That my sweet love would have to be untrue.
Would have to be untrue. Would have to court

Coquettish death, whose impudent and strange
Possessive arms and beauty (of a sort)
Can make a hard man hesitate—and change.
And he will be the one to stammer, "Yes."
Oh mother, mother, where is happiness?

FROM **The Womanhood**

I *the children of the poor*

1

People who have no children can be hard:
Attain a mail of ice and insolence:
Need not pause in the fire, and in no sense
Hesitate in the hurricane to guard.
And when wide world is bitten and bewarred
They perish purely, waving their spirits hence
Without a trace of grace or of offense
To laugh or fail, diffident, wonder-starred.
While through a throttling dark we others hear
The little lifting helplessness, the queer
Whimper-whine; whose unridiculous
Lost softness softly makes a trap for us.
And makes a curse. And makes a sugar of
The malocclusions, the inconditions of love.

What shall I give my children? who are poor,
Who are adjudged the leastwise of the land,
Who are my sweetest lepers, who demand
No velvet and no velvety velour;
But who have begged me for a brisk contour,
Crying that they are quasi, contraband
Because unfinished, graven by a hand
Less than angelic, admirable or sure.
My hand is stuffed with mode, design, device.
But I lack access to my proper stone.
And plenitude of plan shall not suffice
Nor grief nor love shall be enough alone
To ratify my little halves who bear
Across an autumn freezing everywhere.

And shall I prime my children, pray, to pray?
Mites, come invade most frugal vestibules
Spectered with crusts of penitents' renewals
And all hysterics arrogant for a day.
Instruct yourselves here is no devil to pay.
Children, confine your lights in jellied rules;
Resemble graves; be metaphysical mules;
Learn Lord will not distort nor leave the fray.
Behind the scurryings of your neat motif
I shall wait, if you wish: revise the psalm
If that should frighten you: sew up belief
If that should tear: turn, singularly calm
At forehead and at fingers rather wise,
Holding the bandage ready for your eyes.

4

First fight. Then fiddle. Ply the slipping string
With feathery sorcery; muzzle the note
With hurting love; the music that they wrote
Bewitch, bewilder. Qualify to sing
Threadwise. Devise no salt, no hempen thing
For the dear instrument to bear. Devote
The bow to silks and honey. Be remote
A while from malice and from murdering.
But first to arms, to armor. Carry hate
In front of you and harmony behind.
Be deaf to music and to beauty blind.
Win war. Rise bloody, maybe not too late
For having first to civilize a space
Wherein to play your violin with grace.

5

When my dears die, the festival-colored brightness
That is their motion and mild repartee
Enchanted, a macabre mockery
Charming the rainbow radiance into tightness
And into a remarkable politeness
That is not kind and does not want to be,
May not they in the crisp encounter see
Something to recognize and read as rightness?
I say they may, so granitely discreet,
The little crooked questionings inbound,
Concede themselves on most familiar ground,
Cold an old predicament of the breath:
Adroit, the shapely prefaces complete,
Accept the university of death.

VI *the rites for Cousin Vit*

Carried her unprotesting out the door.
Kicked back the casket-stand. But it can't hold her,
That stuff and satin aiming to enfold her,
The lid's contrition nor the bolts before.
Oh oh. Too much. Too much. Even now, surmise,
She rises in the sunshine. There she goes,
Back to the bars she knew and the repose
In love-rooms and the things in people's eyes.
Too vital and too squeaking. Must emerge.
Even now she does the snake-hips with a hiss,
Slops the bad wine across her shantung, talks
Of pregnancy, guitars and bridgework, walks
In parks or alleys, comes haply on the verge
Of happiness, haply hysterics. Is.

VII *I love those little booths at Benvenuti's*

They get to Benvenuti's. There are booths
To hide in while observing tropical truths
About this—dusky folk, so clamorous!
So colorfully incorrect,
So amorous,
So flatly brave!
Boothed-in, one can detect,
Dissect.

One knows and scarcely knows what to expect.

What antics, knives, what lurching dirt; what ditty—
Dirty, rich, carmine, hot, not bottled up,
Straining in sexual soprano, cut
And praying in the bass, partial, unpretty.

They sit, sup,
(Whose friends, if not themselves, arrange
To rent in Venice "a very large cabana,
Small palace," and eat mostly what is strange.)
They sit, they settle; presently are met
By the light heat, the lazy upward whine
And lazy croaky downward drawl of "Tanya."
And their interiors sweat.
They lean back in the half-light, stab their stares
At: walls, panels of imitation oak
With would-be marbly look; linoleum squares
Of dusty rose and brown with little white splashes,
White curls; a vendor tidily encased;
Young yellow waiter moving with straight haste,
Old oaken waiter, lolling and amused;
Some paper napkins in a water glass;
Table, initialed, rubbed, as a desk in school.

They stare. They tire. They feel refused,
Feel overwhelmed by subtle treasons!
Nobody here will take the part of jester.

The absolute stutters, and the rationale
Stoops off in astonishment.
But not gaily
And not with their consent.

They play "They All Say I'm The Biggest Fool"
And "Voo Me On The Vot Nay" and "New Lester
Leaps In" and "For Sentimental Reasons."

But how shall they tell people they have been
Out Bronzeville way? For all the nickels in
Have not bought savagery or defined a "folk."

The colored people will not "clown."

The colored people arrive, sit firmly down,
Eat their Express Spaghetti, their T-bone steak,
Handling their steel and crockery with no clatter,
Laugh punily, rise, go firmly out of the door.

VIII *Beverly Hills, Chicago*
("*and the people live till they have white hair*")
E. M. PRICE

The dry brown coughing beneath their feet,
(Only a while, for the handyman is on his way)
These people walk their golden gardens.
We say ourselves fortunate to be driving by today.

That we may look at them, in their gardens where
The summer ripeness rots. But not raggedly.
Even the leaves fall down in lovelier patterns here.
And the refuse, the refuse is a neat brilliancy.

When they flow sweetly into their houses
With softness and slowness touched by that everlasting
      gold,
We know what they go to. To tea. But that does not
      mean
They will throw some little black dots into some water
      and add sugar and the juice of the cheapest lemons
      that are sold,

While downstairs that woman's vague phonograph
      bleats, "Knock me a kiss."
And the living all to be made again in the sweatingest
      physical manner
Tomorrow. . . . Not that anybody is saying that these
      people have no trouble.
Merely that it is trouble with a gold-flecked beautiful
      banner.

Nobody is saying that these people do not ultimately
      cease to be. And
Sometimes their passings are even more painful than
      ours.
It is just that so often they live till their hair is white.
They make excellent corpses, among the expensive
      flowers. . . .

Nobody is furious. Nobody hates these people.
At least, nobody driving by in this car.
It is only natural, however, that it should occur to us
How much more fortunate they are than we are.

It is only natural that we should look and look
At their wood and brick and stone
And think, while a breath of pine blows,
How different these are from our own.

We do not want them to have less.
But it is only natural that we should think we have not
    enough.
We drive on, we drive on.
When we speak to each other our voices are a little gruff.

XI

One wants a Teller in a time like this.

One's not a man, one's not a woman grown,
To bear enormous business all alone.

One cannot walk this winding street with pride,
Straight-shouldered, tranquil-eyed,
Knowing one knows for sure the way back home.
One wonders if one has a home.

One is not certain if or why or how.
One wants a Teller now:—

Put on your rubbers and you won't catch cold.
Here's hell, there's heaven. Go to Sunday School.
Be patient, time brings all good things—(and cool
Strong balm to calm the burning at the brain?)—
Behold,
Love's true, and triumphs; and God's actual.

XV

Men of careful turns, haters of forks in the road,
The strain at the eye, that puzzlement, that awe—
Grant me that I am human, that I hurt,
That I can cry.

Not that I now ask alms, in shame gone hollow,
Nor cringe outside the loud and sumptuous gate.
Admit me to our mutual estate.

Open my rooms, let in the light and air.
Reserve my service at the human feast.
And let the joy continue. Do not hoard silence
For the moment when I enter, tardily,
To enjoy my height among you. And to love you
No more as a woman loves a drunken mate,
Restraining full caress and good My Dear,
Even pity for the heaviness and the need—
Fearing sudden fire out of the uncaring mouth,
Boiling in the slack eyes, and the traditional blow.
Next, the indifference formal, deep and slow.

Comes in your graceful glider and benign,
To smile upon me bigly; now desires
Me easy, easy; claims the days are softer
Than they were; murmurs reflectively "Remember
When cruelty, metal, public, uncomplex,
Trampled you obviously and every hour. . . ."
(Now cruelty flaunts diplomas, is elite,
Delicate, has polish, knows how to be discreet):
    Requests my patience, wills me to be calm,

Brings me a chair, but the one with broken straw,
Whispers "My friend, no thing is without flaw.
If prejudice is native—and it is—you
Will find it ineradicable—not to
Be juggled, not to be altered at all,
But left unvexed at its place in the properness
Of things, even to be given (with grudging) honor.
    What
We are to hope is that intelligence
Can sugar up our prejudice with politeness.
Politeness will take care of what needs caring.
For the line is there.
And has a meaning. So our fathers said—
And they were wise—we think—At any rate,
They were older than ourselves. And the report is
What's old is wise. At any rate, the line is
Long and electric. Lean beyond and nod.
Be sprightly. Wave. Extend your hand and teeth.
But never forget it stretches there beneath."
The toys are all grotesque
And not for lovely hands; are dangerous,
Serrate in open and artful places. Rise.
Let us combine. There are no magics or elves
Or timely godmothers to guide us. We are lost, must
Wizard a track through our own screaming weed.

Strong Men, Riding Horses

Lester After the Western

Strong Men, riding horses. In the West
On a range five hundred miles. A Thousand. Reaching
From dawn to sunset. Rested blue to orange.
From hope to crying. Except that Strong Men are
Desert-eyed. Except that Strong Men are
Pasted to stars already. Have their cars
Beneath them. Rentless, too. Too broad of chest
To shrink when the Rough Man hails. Too flailing
To redirect the Challenger, when the challenge
Nicks; slams; buttonholes. Too saddled.

I am not like that. I pay rent, am addled
By illegible landlords, run, if robbers call.

What mannerisms I present, employ,
Are camouflage, and what my mouths remark
To word-wall off that broadness of the dark
Is pitiful.
I am not brave at all.

The Bean Eaters

They eat beans mostly, this old yellow pair.
Dinner is a casual affair.
Plain chipware on a plain and creaking wood,
Tin flatware.

Two who are Mostly Good.
Two who have lived their day,
But keep on putting on their clothes
And putting things away.

And remembering . . .
Remembering, with twinklings and twinges,
As they lean over the beans in their rented back room
    that is full of beads and receipts and dolls and
    cloths, tobacco crumbs, vases and fringes.

We Real Cool

The Pool Players.
Seven at the Golden Shovel.

We real cool. We
Left school. We

Lurk late. We
Strike straight. We

Sing sin. We
Thin gin. We

Jazz June. We
Die soon.

Old Mary

My last defense
Is the present tense.

It little hurts me now to know
I shall not go

Cathedral-hunting in Spain
Nor cherrying in Michigan or Maine.

A Bronzeville Mother Loiters in Mississippi. Meanwhile, a Mississippi Mother Burns Bacon

From the first it had been like a
Ballad. It had the beat inevitable. It had the blood.
A wildness cut up, and tied in little bunches,
Like the four-line stanzas of the ballads she had never
       quite
Understood—the ballads they had set her to, in school.

Herself: the milk-white maid, the "maid mild"
Of the ballad. Pursued
By the Dark Villain. Rescued by the Fine Prince.
The Happiness-Ever-After.
That was worth anything.
It was good to be a "maid mild."
That made the breath go fast.

Her bacon burned. She
Hastened to hide it in the step-on can, and
Drew more strips from the meat case. The eggs and
     sour-milk biscuits
Did well. She set out a jar
Of her new quince preserve.

. . . But there was a something about the matter of the
     Dark Villain.
He should have been older, perhaps.
The hacking down of a villain was more fun to think
     about
When his menace possessed undisputed breadth,
     undisputed height,
And a harsh kind of vice.
And best of all, when his history was cluttered
With the bones of many eaten knights and princesses.

The fun was disturbed, then all but nullified
When the Dark Villain was a blackish child
Of fourteen, with eyes still too young to be dirty,
And a mouth too young to have lost every reminder
Of its infant softness.

That boy must have been surprised! For
These were grown-ups. Grown-ups were supposed to
    be wise.
And the Fine Prince—and that other—so tall, so broad,
    so
Grown! Perhaps the boy had never guessed
That the trouble with grown-ups was that under the
    magnificent shell of adulthood, just under,
Waited the baby full of tantrums.
It occurred to her that there may have been something
Ridiculous in the picture of the Fine Prince
Rushing (rich with the breadth and height and
Mature solidness whose lack, in the Dark Villain, was
    impressing her,
Confronting her more and more as this first day after
    the trial
And acquittal wore on) rushing
With his heavy companion to hack down (unhorsed)
That little foe.
So much had happened, she could not remember now
    what that foe had done
Against her, or if anything had been done.
The one thing in the world that she did know and knew
With terrifying clarity was that her composition
Had disintegrated. That, although the pattern prevailed,
The breaks were everywhere. That she could think
Of no thread capable of the necessary
Sew-work.

She made the babies sit in their places at the table.
Then, before calling Him, she hurried

To the mirror with her comb and lipstick. It was
    necessary
To be more beautiful than ever.
The beautiful wife.
For sometimes she fancied he looked at her as though
Measuring her. As if he considered, Had she been
    worth It?
Had *she* been worth the blood, the cramped cries, the
    little stuttering bravado,
The gradual dulling of those Negro eyes,
The sudden, overwhelming *little-boyness* in that barn?
Whatever she might feel or half-feel, the lipstick
    necessity was something apart. He must never
    conclude
That she had not been worth It.

He sat down, the Fine Prince, and
Began buttering a biscuit. He looked at his hands.
He twisted in his chair, he scratched his nose.
He glanced again, almost secretly, at his hands.
More papers were in from the North, he mumbled.
    More meddling headlines.
With their pepper-words, "bestiality," and "barbarism,"
    and
"Shocking."
The half-sneers he had mastered for the trial worked
    across
His sweet and pretty face.

What he'd like to do, he explained, was kill them all.
The time lost. The unwanted fame.

Still, it had been fun to show those intruders
A thing or two. To show that snappy-eyed mother,
That sassy, Northern, brown-black—

Nothing could stop Mississippi.
He knew that. Big Fella
Knew that.
And, what was so good, Mississippi knew that.
Nothing and nothing could stop Mississippi.
They could send in their petitions, and scar
Their newspapers with bleeding headlines. Their
    governors
Could appeal to Washington. . . .

"What I want," the older baby said, "is 'lasses on my
    jam."
Whereupon the younger baby
Picked up the molasses pitcher and threw
The molasses in his brother's face. Instantly
The Fine Prince leaned across the table and slapped
The small and smiling criminal.

She did not speak. When the Hand
Came down and away, and she could look at her child,
At her baby-child,
She could think only of blood.
Surely her baby's cheek
Had disappeared, and in its place, surely,
Hung a heaviness, a lengthening red, a red that had no
    end.
She shook her head. It was not true, of course.

It was not true at all. The
Child's face was as always, the
Color of the paste in her paste-jar.

She left the table, to the tune of the children's
        lamentations, which were shriller
Than ever. She
Looked out of a window. She said not a word. *That*
Was one of the new Somethings—
The fear,
Tying her as with iron.

Suddenly she felt his hands upon her. He had followed
        her
To the window. The children were whimpering now.
Such bits of tots. And she, their mother,
Could not protect them. She looked at her shoulders,
        still
Gripped in the claim of his hands. She tried, but could
        not resist the idea
That a red ooze was seeping, spreading darkly, thickly,
        slowly,
Over her white shoulders, her own shoulders,
And over all of Earth and Mars.

He whispered something to her, did the Fine Prince,
        something
About love, something about love and night and
        intention.

She heard no hoof-beat of the horse and saw no flash of
     the shining steel.

He pulled her face around to meet
His, and there it was, close close,
For the first time in all those days and nights.
His mouth, wet and red,
So very, very, very red,
Closed over hers.

Then a sickness heaved within her. The courtroom
     Coca-Cola,
The courtroom beer and hate and sweat and drone,
Pushed like a wall against her. She wanted to bear it.
But his mouth would not go away and neither would the
Decapitated exclamation points in that Other Woman's
     eyes.

She did not scream.
She stood there.
But a hatred for him burst into glorious flower,
And its perfume enclasped them—big,
Bigger than all magnolias.

The last bleak news of the ballad.
The rest of the rugged music.
The last quatrain.

The Last Quatrain of the
Ballad of Emmett Till

After the Murder,
After the Burial

Emmett's mother is a pretty-faced thing;
      the tint of pulled taffy.
She sits in a red room,
      drinking black coffee.
She kisses her killed boy.
      And she is sorry.
Chaos in windy grays
      through a red prairie.

The Chicago *Defender* Sends
a Man to Little Rock

Fall, 1957

In Little Rock the people bear
Babes, and comb and part their hair
And watch the want ads, put repair
To roof and latch. While wheat toast burns
A woman waters multiferns.

Time upholds or overturns
The many, tight, and small concerns.

In Little Rock the people sing
Sunday hymns like anything,
Through Sunday pomp and polishing.

And after testament and tunes,
Some soften Sunday afternoons
With lemon tea and Lorna Doones.

I forecast
And I believe
Come Christmas Little Rock will cleave
To Christmas tree and trifle, weave,
From laugh and tinsel, texture fast.

In Little Rock is baseball; Barcarolle.
That hotness in July . . . the uniformed figures raw and
        implacable
And not intellectual,
Batting the hotness or clawing the suffering dust.
The Open Air Concert, on the special twilight green . . .
When Beethoven is brutal or whispers to lady-like air.
Blanket-sitters are solemn, as Johann troubles to lean
To tell them what to mean. . . .

There is love, too, in Little Rock. Soft women softly
Opening themselves in kindness,
Or, pitying one's blindness,
Awaiting one's pleasure
In azure
Glory with anguished rose at the root. . . .
To wash away old semi-discomfitures.
They re-teach purple and unsullen blue.
The wispy soils go. And uncertain
Half-havings have they clarified to sures.

In Little Rock they know
Not answering the telephone is a way of rejecting life,
That it is our business to be bothered, is our business
To cherish bores or boredom, be polite
To lies and love and many-faceted fuzziness.

I scratch my head, massage the hate-I-had.
I blink across my prim and pencilled pad.
The saga I was sent for is not down.
Because there is a puzzle in this town.
The biggest News I do not dare
Telegraph to the Editor's chair:
"They are like people everywhere."

The angry Editor would reply
In hundred harryings of Why.

And true, they are hurling spittle, rock,
Garbage and fruit in Little Rock.
And I saw coiling storm a-writhe
On bright madonnas. And a scythe
Of men harassing brownish girls.
(The bows and barrettes in the curls
And braids declined away from joy.)

I saw a bleeding brownish boy. . . .

The lariat lynch-wish I deplored.

The loveliest lynchee was our Lord.

The Lovers of the Poor

           arrive. The Ladies from the Ladies' Betterment
               League
Arrive in the afternoon, the late light slanting
In diluted gold bars across the boulevard brag
Of proud, seamed faces with mercy and murder hinting
Here, there, interrupting, all deep and debonair,
The pink paint on the innocence of fear;
Walk in a gingerly manner up the hall.
Cutting with knives served by their softest care,
Served by their love, so barbarously fair.
Whose mothers taught: You'd better not be cruel!
You had better not throw stones upon the wrens!
Herein they kiss and coddle and assault
Anew and dearly in the innocence
With which they baffle nature. Who are full,
Sleek, tender-clad, fit, fiftyish, a-glow, all
Sweetly abortive, hinting at fat fruit,
Judge it high time that fiftyish fingers felt
Beneath the lovelier planes of enterprise.
To resurrect. To moisten with milky chill.
To be a random hitching post or plush.
To be, for wet eyes, random and handy hem.
           Their guild is giving money to the poor.
The worthy poor. The very very worthy
And beautiful poor. Perhaps just not too swarthy?
Perhaps just not too dirty nor too dim
Nor—passionate. In truth, what they could wish
Is—something less than derelict or dull.
Not staunch enough to stab, though, gaze for gaze!

God shield them sharply from the beggar-bold!
The noxious needy ones whose battle's bald
Nonetheless for being voiceless, hits one down.
        But it's all so bad! and entirely too much for them.
The stench; the urine, cabbage, and dead beans,
Dead porridges of assorted dusty grains,
The old smoke, *heavy* diapers, and, they're told,
Something called chitterlings. The darkness. Drawn
Darkness, or dirty light. The soil that stirs.
The soil that looks the soil of centuries.
And for that matter the *general* oldness. Old
Wood. Old marble. Old tile. Old old old.
Not homekind Oldness! Not Lake Forest, Glencoe.
Nothing is sturdy, nothing is majestic,
There is no quiet drama, no rubbed glaze, no
Unkillable infirmity of such
A tasteful turn as lately they have left,
Glencoe, Lake Forest, and to which their cars
Must presently restore them. When they're done
With dullards and distortions of this fistic
Patience of the poor and put-upon.
        They've never seen such a make-do-ness as
Newspaper rugs before! In this, this "flat,"
Their hostess is gathering up the oozed, the rich
Rugs of the morning (tattered! the bespattered . . .),
Readies to spread clean rugs for afternoon.
Here is a scene for you. The Ladies look,
In horror, behind a substantial citizeness
Whose trains clank out across her swollen heart.
Who, arms akimbo, almost fills a door.
All tumbling children, quilts dragged to the floor

And tortured thereover, potato peelings, soft-
Eyed kitten, hunched-up, haggard, to-be-hurt.
      Their League is allotting largesse to the Lost.
But to put their clean, their pretty money, to put
Their money collected from delicate rose-fingers
Tipped with their hundred flawless rose-nails seems . . .
      They own Spode, Lowestoft, candelabra,
Mantels, and hostess gowns, and sunburst clocks,
Turtle soup, Chippendale, red satin "hangings,"
Aubussons and Hattie Carnegie. They Winter
In Palm Beach; cross the Water in June; attend,
When suitable, the nice Art Institute;
Buy the right books in the best bindings; saunter
On Michigan, Easter mornings, in sun or wind.
Oh Squalor! This sick four-story hulk, this fibre
With fissures everywhere! Why, what are bringings
Of loathe-love largesse? What shall peril hungers
So old old, what shall flatter the desolate?
Tin can, blocked fire escape and chitterling
And swaggering seeking youth and the puzzled
      wreckage
Of the middle passage, and urine and stale shames
And, again, the porridges of the underslung
And children children children. Heavens! That
Was a rat, surely, off there, in the shadows? Long
And long-tailed? Gray? The Ladies from the Ladies'
Betterment League agree it will be better
To achieve the outer air that rights and steadies,
To hie to a house that does not holler, to ring
Bells elsetime, better presently to cater
To no more Possibilities, to get

Away. Perhaps the money can be posted.
Perhaps they two may choose another Slum!
Some serious sooty half-unhappy home!—
Where loathe-love likelier may be invested.
          Keeping their scented bodies in the center
Of the hall as they walk down the hysterical hall,
They allow their lovely skirts to graze no wall,
Are off at what they manage of a canter,
And, resuming all the clues of what they were,
Try to avoid inhaling the laden air.

The Crazy Woman

I shall not sing a May song.
A May song should be gay.
I'll wait until November
And sing a song of gray.

I'll wait until November.
That is the time for me.
I'll go out in the frosty dark
And sing most terribly.

And all the little people
Will stare at me and say,
"That is the Crazy Woman
Who would not sing in May."

A Lovely Love

Lillian's

Let it be alleys. Let it be a hall
Whose janitor javelins epithet and thought
To cheapen hyacinth darkness that we sought
And played we found, rot, make the petals fall.
Let it be stairways, and a splintery box
Where you have thrown me, scraped me with your kiss,
Have honed me, have released me after this
Cavern kindness, smiled away our shocks.
That is the birthright of our lovely love
In swaddling clothes. Not like that Other one.
Not lit by any fondling star above.
Not found by any wise men, either. Run.
People are coming. They must not catch us here
Definitionless in this strict atmosphere.

Bronzeville Woman in a Red Hat

Hires out to Mrs. Miles

I

They had never had one in the house before.

    The strangeness of it all. Like unleashing
A lion, really. Poised
To pounce. A puma. A panther. A black
Bear.
There it stood in the door,
Under a red hat that was rash, but refreshing—

In a tasteless way, of course—across the dull dare,
The semi-assault of that extraordinary blackness.
The slackness
Of that light pink mouth told little. The eyes told of
       heavy care. . . .
But that was neither here nor there,
And nothing to a wage-paying mistress as should
Be getting her due whether life had been good
For her slave, or bad.
There it stood
In the door. They had never had
One in the house before.

But the Irishwoman had left!
A message had come.
Something about a murder at home.
A daughter's husband—"berserk," that was the phrase:
The dear man had "gone berserk"
And short work—
With a hammer—had been made
Of this daughter and her nights and days.
The Irishwoman (underpaid,
Mrs. Miles remembered with smiles),
Who was a perfect jewel, a red-faced trump,
A good old sort, a baker
Of rum cake, a maker
Of Mustard, would never return.
Mrs. Miles had begged the bewitched woman
To finish, at least, the biscuit blending,
To tarry till the curry was done,
To show some concern

For the burning soup, to attend to the tending
Of the tossed salad. "Inhuman,"
Patsy Houlihan had called Mrs. Miles.
"Inhuman." And "a fool."
And "a cool
One."
The Alert Agency had leafed through its files—
On short notice could offer
Only this dusky duffer
That now made its way to her kitchen and sat on her
kitchen stool.

II

Her creamy child kissed by the black maid! square on
the mouth!
World yelled, world writhed, world turned to light and
rolled
Into her kitchen, nearly knocked her down.

Quotations, of course, from baby books were great
Ready armor; (but her animal distress
Wore, too and under, a subtler metal dress,
Inheritance of approximately hate).
Say baby shrieked to see his finger bleed,
Wished human humoring—there was a kind
Of unintimate love, a love more of the mind
To order the nebulousness of that need.
—This was the way to put it, this the relief.
This sprayed a honey upon marvelous grime.
This told it possible to postpone the reef.
Fashioned a huggable darling out of crime.

Made monster personable in personal sight
By cracking mirrors down the personal night.
Disgust crawled through her as she chased the theme.
She, quite supposing purity despoiled,
Committed to sourness, disordered, soiled,
Went in to pry the ordure from the cream.
Cooing, "Come." (Come out of the cannibal wilderness,
Dirt, dark, into the sun and bloomful air.
Return to freshness of your right world, wear
Sweetness again. Be done with beast, duress.)

Child with continuing cling issued his No in final fire,
        Kissed back the colored maid,
        Not wise enough to freeze or be afraid.
        Conscious of kindness, easy creature bond.
        Love had been handy and rapid to respond.

Heat at the hairline, heat between the bowels,
Examining seeming coarse unnatural scene,
She saw all things except herself serene:
Child, big black woman, pretty kitchen towels.

Bessie of Bronzeville Visits Mary and Norman at a Beach-house in New Buffalo

You said, "Now take your shoes off," while what played
Was not the back-town boogie but a green
Wet music stuff, above the wide and clean
Sand, and my hand laughed.
Toes urged the slab to amber foam.

And I was hurt by cider in the air.
And what the lake-wash did was dizzying.
I thought of England, as I watched you bring
The speckled pebbles,
The smooth quartz; I thought of Italy.

Italy and England come.
A sea sits up and starts to sing to me.

The Ballad of Rudolph Reed

Rudolph Reed was oaken.
His wife was oaken too.
And his two good girls and his good little man
Oakened as they grew.

"I am not hungry for berries.
I am not hungry for bread.
But hungry hungry for a house
Where at night a man in bed

"May never hear the plaster
Stir as if in pain.
May never hear the roaches
Falling like fat rain.

"Where never wife and children need
Go blinking through the gloom.
Where every room of many rooms
Will be full of room.

"Oh my home may have its east or west
Or north or south behind it.
All I know is I shall know it,
And fight for it when I find it."

It was in a street of bitter white
That he made his application.
For Rudolph Reed was oakener
Than others in the nation.

The agent's steep and steady stare
Corroded to a grin.
Why, you black old, tough old hell of a man,
Move your family in!

Nary a grin grinned Rudolph Reed,
Nary a curse cursed he,
But moved in his House. With his dark little wife,
And his dark little children three.

A neighbor would *look*, with a yawning eye
That squeezed into a slit.
But the Rudolph Reeds and the children three
Were too joyous to notice it.

For were they not firm in a home of their own
With windows everywhere
And a beautiful banistered stair
And a front yard for flowers and a back yard for grass?

The first night, a rock, big as two fists.
The second, a rock big as three.
But nary a curse cursed Rudolph Reed.
(Though oaken as man could be.)

The third night, a silvery ring of glass.
Patience ached to endure.
But he looked, and lo! small Mabel's blood
Was staining her gaze so pure.

Then up did rise our Rudolph Reed
And pressed the hand of his wife,
And went to the door with a thirty-four
And a beastly butcher knife.

He ran like a mad thing into the night.
And the words in his mouth were stinking.
By the time he had hurt his first white man
He was no longer thinking.

By the time he had hurt his fourth white man
Rudolph Reed was dead.
His neighbors gathered and kicked his corpse.
"Nigger—" his neighbors said.

Small Mabel whimpered all night long,
For calling herself the cause.
Her oak-eyed mother did no thing
But change the bloody gauze.

The Egg Boiler

Being you, you cut your poetry from wood.
The boiling of an egg is heavy art.
You come upon it as an artist should,
With rich-eyed passion, and with straining heart.
We fools, we cut our poems out of air,
Night color, wind soprano, and such stuff.
And sometimes weightlessness is much to bear.
You mock it, though, you name it Not Enough.
The egg, spooned gently to the avid pan,
And left the strict three minutes, or the four,
Is your Enough and art for any man.
We fools give courteous ear—then cut some more,
Shaping a gorgeous Nothingness from cloud.
You watch us, eat your egg, and laugh aloud.

A Catch of Shy Fish

garbageman: the man with the orderly mind

What do you think of us in fuzzy endeavor, you whose
    directions are sterling, whose lunge is straight?
Can you make a reason, how can you pardon us who
    memorize the rules and never score?
Who memorize the rules from your own text but never
    quite transfer them to the game,
Who never quite receive the whistling ball, who gawk,
    begin to absorb the crowd's own roar.

Is earnestness enough, may earnestness attract or lead to
    light;
Is light enough, if hands in clumsy frenzy, flimsy
    whimsicality, enlist;
Is light enough when this bewilderment crying against
    the dark shuts down the shades?
    Dilute confusion. Find and explode our mist.

sick man looks at flowers

You are sick and old, and there is a closing in—
The eyes gone dead to all that would beguile.

Echoes are dull and the body accepts no touch
Except its pain. Mind is a little isle.

But now invades this impudence of red!
This ripe rebuke, this burgeoning affluence
Mocks me and mocks the desert of my bed.

old people working (garden, car)

Old people working. Making a gift of garden.
Or washing a car, so some one else may ride.
A note of alliance, an eloquence of pride.
A way of greeting or sally to the world.

weaponed woman

Well, life has been a baffled vehicle
And baffling. But she fights, and
Has fought, according to her lights and
The lenience of her whirling-place.

She fights with semi-folded arms,
Her strong bag, and the stiff
Frost of her face (that challenges "When" and "If.")
And altogether she does Rather Well.

old tennis player

Refuses
To refuse the racket, to mutter No to the net.
He leans to life, conspires to give and get
Other serving yet.

a surrealist and Omega

Omega ran to witness him; beseeched;
Brought caution and carnality and cash.
She sauced him brownly, eating him
Under her fancy's finest Worcestershire.

He zigzagged.
He was a knotted hiss.
He was an insane hash
Of rebellious small strengths
And soft-mouthed mumbling weakness.

The art
Would not come right. That smear,
That yellow in the gray corner—
That was not right, he had not reached
The right, the careless flailed-out bleakness.

A god, a child.
He said he was most seriously amiss.

She had no purple or pearl to hang
About the neck of one a-wild.

A bantam beauty
Loving his ownhood for all it was worth.

Spaulding and François

There are cloudlets and things of cool silver in our
        dream, there are all of the Things Ethereal.
There is a
Scent of wind cut with pine, a noise of
Wind tangled among bells. There is spiritual laughter
Too hushed to be gay, too high: the happiness
Of angels. And there are angels' eyes, soft,
Heavy with precious compulsion.

But the People
Will not let us alone; will not credit, condone
Art-loves that shun
Them (moderate Christians rotting in the sun.)

Big Bessie throws her son into the street

A day of sunny face and temper.
The winter trees
Are musical.

Bright lameness from my beautiful disease,
You have your destiny to chip and eat.

Be precise.
With something better than candles in the eyes.
(Candles are not enough.)

At the root of the will, a wild inflammable stuff.

New pioneer of days and ways, be gone.
Hunt out your own or make your own alone.

Go down the street.

Boy Breaking Glass

To Marc Crawford
from whom the commission

Whose broken window is a cry of art
(success, that winks aware
as elegance, as a treasonable faith)
is raw: is sonic: is old-eyed première.
Our beautiful flaw and terrible ornament.
Our barbarous and metal little man.

"I shall create! If not a note, a hole.
If not an overture, a desecration."

Full of pepper and light
and Salt and night and cargoes.

"Don't go down the plank
if you see there's no extension.
Each to his grief, each to
his loneliness and fidgety revenge.
Nobody knew where I was and now I am no longer
    there."

The only sanity is a cup of tea.
The music is in minors.

Each one other
is having different weather.

"It was you, it was you who threw away my name!
And this is everything I have for me."

Who has not Congress, lobster, love, luau,
the Regency Room, the Statue of Liberty,
runs. A sloppy amalgamation.
A mistake.
A cliff.
A hymn, a snare, and an exceeding sun.

Medgar Evers

For Charles Evers

The man whose height his fear improved he
arranged to fear no further. The raw
intoxicated time was time for better birth or
a final death.

Old styles, old tempos, all the engagement of
the day—the sedate, the regulated fray—
the antique light, the Moral rose, old gusts,
tight whistlings from the past, the mothballs
in the Love at last our man forswore.

Medgar Evers annoyed confetti and assorted
brands of businessmen's eyes.

The shows came down: to maxims and surprise.
And palsy.

Roaring no rapt arise-ye to the dead, he
leaned across tomorrow. People said that
he was holding clean globes in his hands.

Malcolm X

For Dudley Randall

Original.
Ragged-round.
Rich-robust.

He had the hawk-man's eyes.
We gasped. We saw the maleness.
The maleness raking out and making guttural the air
and pushing us to walls.

And in a soft and fundamental hour
a sorcery devout and vertical
beguiled the world.

He opened us—
who was a key,

who was a man.

Two Dedications

I   The Chicago Picasso
August 15, 1967

"Mayor Daley tugged a white ribbon, loosing the blue percale
wrap. A hearty cheer went up as the covering slipped off the big
steel sculpture that looks at once like a bird and a woman."
—Chicago *Sun-Times*

(Seiji Ozawa leads the Symphony.
The Mayor smiles.
And 50,000 See.)

Does man love Art? Man visits Art, but squirms.
Art hurts. Art urges voyages—
and it is easier to stay at home,
the nice beer ready.
     In commonrooms
we belch, or sniff, or scratch.
Are raw.

But we must cook ourselves and style ourselves for Art,
          who
is a requiring courtesan.
We squirm.
We do not hug the Mona Lisa.
We
may touch or tolerate
an astounding fountain, or a horse-and-rider.
At most, another Lion.

Observe the tall cold of a Flower
which is as innocent and as guilty,
as meaningful and as meaningless as any
other flower in the western field.

II *The Wall*

August 27, 1967

For Edward Christmas

"The side wall of a typical slum building on the corner of 43rd
and Langley became a mural communicating black dignity. . . ."
—*Ebony*

A drumdrumdrum.
Humbly we come.
South of success and east of gloss and glass are
sandals;
flowercloth;
grave hoops of wood or gold, pendant
from black ears, brown ears, reddish-brown
and ivory ears;

black boy-men.
Black
boy-men on roofs fist out "Black Power!" Val,
a little black stampede
in African
images of brass and flowerswirl,
fists out "Black Power!"—tightens pretty eyes,
leans back on mothercountry and is tract,
is treatise through her perfect and tight teeth.

Women in wool hair chant their poetry.
Phil Cohran gives us messages and music
made of developed bone and polished and honed cult.
It is the Hour of tribe and of vibration,
the day-long Hour. It is the Hour
of ringing, rouse, of ferment-festival.

On Forty-third and Langley
black furnaces resent ancient
legislatures
of ploy and scruple and practical gelatin.
They keep the fever in,
fondle the fever.

All
worship the Wall.

I mount the rattling wood. Walter
says, "She is good." Says, "She
our Sister is." In front of me
hundreds of faces, red-brown, brown, black, ivory,
yield me hot trust, their yea and their Announcement
that they are ready to rile the high-flung ground.
Behind me, Paint.
Heroes.
No child has defiled
the Heroes of this Wall this serious Appointment
this still Wing
this Scald this Flute this heavy Light this Hinge.

An emphasis is paroled.
The old decapitations are revised,
the dispossessions beakless.

And we sing.

The Blackstone Rangers

I   *As Seen by Disciplines*

There they are.
Thirty at the corner.
Black, raw, ready.
Sores in the city
that do not want to heal.

II   *The Leaders*

Jeff. Gene. Geronimo. And Bop.
They cancel, cure and curry.
Hardly the dupes of the downtown thing
the cold bonbon,
the rhinestone thing. And hardly
in a hurry.
Hardly Belafonte, King,
Black Jesus, Stokely, Malcolm X or Rap.
Bungled trophies.
Their country is a Nation on no map.

Jeff, Gene, Geronimo and Bop
in the passionate noon,
in bewitching night
are the detailed men, the copious men.
They curry, cure,
they cancel, cancelled images whose Concerts
are not divine, vivacious; the different tins
are intense last entries; pagan argument;
translations of the night.

The Blackstone bitter bureaus
(bureaucracy is footloose) edit, fuse
unfashionable damnations and descent;
and exulting, monstrous hand on monstrous hand,
construct, strangely, a monstrous pearl or grace.

III   *Gang Girls*
A Rangerette

Gang Girls are sweet exotics.
Mary Ann
uses the nutrients of her orient,
but sometimes sighs for Cities of blue and jewel
beyond her Ranger rim of Cottage Grove.
(Bowery Boys, Disciples, Whip-Birds will
dissolve no margins, stop no savory sanctities.)

Mary is
a rose in a whiskey glass.

Mary's
Februaries shudder and are gone. Aprils
fret frankly, lilac hurries on.
Summer is a hard irregular ridge.
October looks away.
And that's the Year!

           Save for her bugle-love.
Save for the bleat of not-obese devotion.
Save for Somebody Terribly Dying, under
the philanthropy of robins. Save for her Ranger
bringing
an amount of rainbow in a string-drawn bag.
"Where did you get the diamond?" Do not ask:
but swallow, straight, the spirals of his flask
and assist him at your zipper; pet his lips
and help him clutch you.

Love's another departure.
Will there be any arrivals, confirmations?
Will there be gleaning?

Mary, the Shakedancer's child
from the rooming-flat, pants carefully, peers at
her laboring lover. . . .
           Mary! Mary Ann!
Settle for sandwiches! settle for stocking caps!
for sudden blood, aborted carnival,
the props and niceties of non-loneliness—
the rhymes of Leaning.

The Sermon on the Warpland

*"The fact that we are black
is our ultimate reality."*
　　　　—RON KARENGA

And several strengths from drowsiness campaigned
but spoke in Single Sermon on the warpland.

And went about the warpland saying No.
"My people, black and black, revile the River.
Say that the River turns, and turn the River.

Say that our Something in doublepod contains
seeds for the coming hell and health together.
Prepare to meet
(sisters, brothers) the brash and terrible weather;
the pains;
the bruising; the collapse of bestials, idols.
But then oh then!—the stuffing of the hulls!
the seasoning of the perilously sweet!
the health! the heralding of the clear obscure!

Build now your Church, my brothers, sisters. Build
never with brick nor Corten nor with granite.
Build with lithe love. With love like lion-eyes.
With love like morningrise.
With love like black, our black—
luminously indiscreet;
complete; continuous."

The Second Sermon on the Warpland

For Walter Bradford

1.

This is the urgency: Live!
and have your blooming in the noise of the whirlwind.

2.

Salve salvage in the spin.
Endorse the splendor splashes;
stylize the flawed utility;
prop a malign or failing light—
but know the whirlwind is our commonwealth.
Not the easy man, who rides above them all,
not the jumbo brigand,
not the pet bird of poets, that sweetest sonnet,
shall straddle the whirlwind.
Nevertheless, live.

3.

All about are the cold places,
all about are the pushmen and jeopardy, theft—
all about are the stormers and scramblers but
what must our Season be, which starts from Fear?
Live and go out.
Define and
medicate the whirlwind.

4.

The time
cracks into furious flower. Lifts its face

all unashamed. And sways in wicked grace.
Whose half-black hands assemble oranges
is tom-tom hearted
(goes in bearing oranges and boom).
And there are bells for orphans—
and red and shriek and sheen.
A garbageman is dignified
as any diplomat.
Big Bessie's feet hurt like nobody's business,
but she stands—bigly—under the unruly scrutiny, stands
      in the wild weed.

In the wild weed
she is a citizen,
and is a moment of highest quality; admirable.

It is lonesome, yes. For we are the last of the loud.
Nevertheless, live.

Conduct your blooming in the noise and whip of the
      whirlwind.

Riot

A riot is the language of the unheard.
            —MARTIN LUTHER KING

John Cabot, out of Wilma, once a Wycliffe,
all whitebluerose below his golden hair,
wrapped richly in right linen and right wool,
almost forgot his Jaguar and Lake Bluff;
almost forgot Grandtully (which is The
Best Thing That Ever Happened To Scotch); almost
forgot the sculpture at the Richard Gray
and Distelheim; the kidney pie at Maxim's,
the Grenadine de Boeuf at Maison Henri.

Because the Negroes were coming down the street.

Because the Poor were sweaty and unpretty
(not like Two Dainty Negroes in Winnetka)
and they were coming toward him in rough ranks.
In seas. In windsweep. They were black and loud.
And not detainable. And not discreet.

Gross. Gross. *"Que tu es grossier!"* John Cabot
itched instantly beneath the nourished white
that told his story of glory to the World.

"Don't let It touch me! the blackness! Lord!" he
      whispered
to any handy angel in the sky.

But, in a thrilling announcement, on It drove
and breathed on him: and touched him. In that breath
the fume of pig foot, chitterling and cheap chili,
malign, mocked John. And, in terrific touch, old
averted doubt jerked forward decently,
cried "Cabot! John! You are a desperate man,
and the desperate die expensively today."

John Cabot went down in the smoke and fire
and broken glass and blood, and he cried "Lord!
Forgive these nigguhs that know not what they do."

The Third Sermon on the Warpland

Phoenix
"In Egyptian mythology, a bird which lived for five
hundred years and then consumed itself in fire, rising
renewed from the ashes."
                                                —WEBSTER

The earth is a beautiful place.
Watermirrors and things to be reflected.
Goldenrod across the little lagoon.

The Black Philosopher says
"Our chains are in the keep of the Keeper

in a labeled cabinet
on the second shelf by the cookies,
sonatas, the arabesques . . . .
There's a rattle, sometimes.
You do not hear it who mind only
cookies and crunch them.
You do not hear the remarkable music—'A
Death Song For You Before You Die.'
If you could hear it
you would make music too.
The *black*blues."

———

West Madison Street.
In "Jessie's Kitchen"
nobody's eating Jessie's Perfect Food.
Crazy flowers
cry up across the sky, spreading
and hissing *This is*
it.

———

The young men run.

They will not steal Bing Crosby but will steal
Melvin Van Peebles who made Lillie
a thing of Zampoughi a thing of red wiggles and trebles
(and I know there are twenty wire stalks sticking out of
    her head
as her underfed haunches jerk jazz.)

———

A clean riot is not one in which little rioters
long-stomped, long-straddled, BEANLESS
but knowing no Why
go steal in hell
a radio, sit to hear James Brown
and Mingus, Young-Holt, Coleman, John, on V.O.N.
and sun themselves in Sin.

However, what
is going on
is going on.

———

Fire.
That is their way of lighting candles in the darkness.
A White Philosopher said
'It is better to light one candle than curse the darkness.'
          These candles curse—
inverting the deeps of the darkness.

GUARD HERE, GUNS LOADED.
The young men run.
The children in ritual chatter
scatter upon
their Own and old geography.

The Law comes sirening across the town.

———

A woman is dead.
Motherwoman.
She lies among the boxes

(that held the haughty hats, the Polish sausages)
in newish, thorough, firm virginity
as rich as fudge is if you've had five pieces.
Not again shall she
partake of steak
on Christmas mornings, nor of nighttime
chicken and wine at Val Gray Ward's
nor say
of Mr. Beetley, Exit Jones, Junk Smith
nor neat New-baby Williams (man-to-many)
"He treat me right."

That was a gut gal.

"We'll do an us!" yells Yancey, a twittering twelve.
"Instead of your deathintheafternoon,
kill 'em, bull!
kill 'em, bull!"

The Black Philosopher blares
"I tell you, ex*haustive* black integrity
would assure a blackless America. . . ."

———

Nine die, Sun-Times will tell
and will tell too
in small black-bordered oblongs *"Rumor? check it
at 744-4111."*

———

A Poem to Peanut.
"Cooooooool!" purrs Peanut. Peanut is
Richard—a Ranger and a gentleman.

A Signature. A Herald. And a Span.
This Peanut will not let his men explode.
And Rico will not.
Neither will Sengali.
Nor Bop nor Jeff, Geronimo nor Lover.
These merely peer and purr,
and pass the Passion over.
The Disciples stir
and thousandfold confer
with ranging Rangermen;
mutual in their "Yeah!—
this AIN'T all upinheah!"

———

"But WHY do These People offend *themselves*?"
    say they
who say also "It's time.
It's time to help
These People."

———

Lies are told and legends made.
Phoenix rises unafraid.

The Black Philosopher will remember:
"There they came to life and exulted,
the hurt mute.
Then it was over.

The dust, as they say, settled."

The Life of Lincoln West

Ugliest little boy
that everyone ever saw.
That is what everyone said.

Even to his mother it was apparent—
when the blue-aproned nurse came into the
northeast end of the maternity ward
bearing his squeals and plump bottom
looped up in a scant receiving blanket,
bending, to pass the bundle carefully
into the waiting mother-hands—that this
was no cute little ugliness, no sly baby
    waywardness
that was going to inch away
as would baby fat, baby curl, and
baby spot-rash. The pendulous lip, the
branching ears, the eyes so wide and wild,
the vague unvibrant brown of the skin,
and, most disturbing, the great head.
These components of That Look bespoke
the sure fibre. The deep grain.

His father could not bear the sight of him.
His mother high-piled her pretty dyed hair and
put him among her hairpins and sweethearts,
dance slippers, torn paper roses.
He was not less than these,
he was not more.

As the little Lincoln grew,
uglily upward and out, he began
to understand that something was
wrong. His little ways of trying
to please his father, the bringing
of matches, the jumping aside at
warning sound of oh-so-large and
rushing stride, the smile that gave
and gave and gave—Unsuccessful!

Even Christmases and Easters were spoiled.
He would be sitting at the
family feasting table, really
delighting in the displays of mashed potatoes
and the rich golden
fat-crust of the ham or the festive
fowl, when he would look up and find
somebody feeling indignant about him.

What a pity what a pity. No love
for one so loving. The little Lincoln
loved Everybody. Ants. The changing
caterpillar. His much-missing mother.
His kindergarten teacher.

His kindergarten teacher—whose
concern for him was composed of one
part sympathy and two parts repulsion.
The others ran up with their little drawings.
He ran up with his.
She
tried to be as pleasant with him as
with others, but it was difficult.
For she was all pretty! all daintiness,
all tiny vanilla, with blue eyes and fluffy
sun-hair. One afternoon she
saw him in the hall looking bleak against
the wall. It was strange because the
bell had long since rung and no other
child was in sight. Pity flooded her.
She buttoned her gloves and suggested
cheerfully that she walk him home. She
started out bravely, holding him by the
hand. But she had not walked far before
she regretted it. The little monkey.
Must everyone look? And clutching her
hand like that . . . Literally pinching
it. . .

At seven, the little Lincoln loved
the brother and sister who
moved next door. Handsome. Well-
dressed. Charitable, often, to him. They
enjoyed him because he was
resourceful, made up
games, told stories. But when

their More Acceptable friends came they turned
their handsome backs on him. He
hated himself for his feeling
of well-being when with them despite—
Everything.

He spent much time looking at himself
in mirrors. What could be done?
But there was no
shrinking his head. There was no
binding his ears.

"Don't touch me!" cried the little
fairy-like being in the playground.

Her name was Nerissa. The many
children were playing tag, but when
he caught her, she recoiled, jerked free
and ran. It was like all the
rainbow that ever was, going off
forever, all, all the sparklings in
the sunset west.

One day, while he was yet seven,
a thing happened. In the down-town movies
with his mother a white
man in the seat beside him whispered
loudly to a companion, and pointed at
the little Linc.
"THERE! That's the kind I've been wanting
to show you! One of the best

examples of the specie. Not like
those diluted Negroes you see so much of on
the streets these days, but the
real thing.

Black, ugly, and odd. You
can see the savagery. The blunt
blankness. That is the real
thing."

His mother—her hair had never looked so
red around the dark brown
velvet of her face—jumped up,
shrieked "Go to ——" She did not finish.
She yanked to his feet the little
Lincoln, who was sitting there
staring in fascination at his assessor. At the author of his
new idea.

All the way home he was happy. Of course,
he had not liked the word
"ugly."
But, after, should he not
be used to that by now? What had
struck him, among words and meanings
he could little understand, was the phrase
"the real thing."
He didn't know quite why,
but he liked that.
He liked that very much.

When he was hurt, too much
stared at—
too much
left alone—he
thought about that. He told himself
"After all, I'm
the real thing."

It comforted him.

To Don at Salaam

I like to see you lean back in your chair
so far you have to fall but do not—
your arms back, your fine hands
in your print pockets.

Beautiful. Impudent.
Ready for life.
A tied storm.

I like to see you wearing your boy smile
whose tribute is for two of us or three.

Sometimes in life
things seem to be moving
and they are not
and they are not
there.
You are there.

Your voice is the listened-for music.
Your act is the consolidation.

I like to see you living in the world.

Paul Robeson

That time
we all heard it,
cool and clear,
cutting across the hot grit of the day.
The major Voice.
The adult Voice
forgoing Rolling River,
forgoing tearful tale of bale and barge
and other symptoms of an old despond.
Warning, in music-words
devout and large,
that we are each other's
harvest:
we are each other's
business:
we are each other's
magnitude and bond.

The Boy Died in My Alley

to Running Boy

The Boy died in my alley
without my Having Known.
Policeman said, next morning,
"Apparently died Alone."

"You heard a shot?" Policeman said.
Shots I hear and Shots I hear.
I never see the Dead.

The Shot that killed him yes I heard
as I heard the Thousand shots before;
careening tinnily down the nights
across my years and arteries.

Policeman pounded on my door.
"Who is it?" "POLICE!" Policeman yelled.
"A Boy was dying in your alley.
A Boy is dead, and in your alley.
And have you known this Boy before?"

I have known this Boy before.
I have known this Boy before, who

ornaments my alley.
I never saw his face at all.
I never saw his futurefall.
But I have known this Boy.

I have always heard him deal with death.
I have always heard the shout, the volley.
I have closed my heart-ears late and early.
And I have killed him ever.

I joined the Wild and killed him
with knowledgeable unknowing.
I saw where he was going.
I saw him Crossed. And seeing,
I did not take him down.

He cried not only "Father!"
but "Mother!
Sister!
Brother."
The cry climbed up the alley.
It went up to the wind.
It hung upon the heaven
for a long
stretch-strain of Moment.

The red floor of my alley
is a special speech to me.

Steam Song

Hostilica hears Al Green

That Song it sing the sweetness
like a good Song can,
and make a woman want to
run out and find her man.

Ain got no pretty mansion.
Ain got no ruby ring.
My man is my only
necessary thing.

That Song boil up my blood
like a good Song can.
It make this woman want to
run out and find her man.

Elegy in a Rainbow

Moe Belle's double love song.

When I was a little girl
   Christmas was exquisite.
   I didn't touch it.
I didn't look at it too closely.
   To do that to do that
might nullify the shine.

Thus with a Love
that has to have a Home
like the Black Nation,
like the Black Nation
defining its own Roof
that no one else can see.

Primer for Blacks

Blackness
is a title,
is a preoccupation,
is a commitment Blacks
are to comprehend—
and in which you are
to perceive your Glory.

The conscious shout
of all that is white is
"It's Great to be white."
The conscious shout
of the slack in Black is
"It's Great to be white."
Thus all that is white
has white strength and yours.

The word Black
has geographic power,
pulls everybody in:
Blacks here—
Blacks there—
Blacks wherever they may be.

And remember, you Blacks, what they told you—
remember your Education:
"one Drop—one Drop
maketh a brand new Black."
　　　Oh mighty Drop.
—— And because they have given us kindly
so many more of our people
Blackness
stretches over the land.
Blackness—
the Black of it,
the rust-red of it,
the milk and cream of it,
the tan and yellow-tan of it,
the deep-brown middle-brown high-brown of it,
the "olive" and ochre of it—
Blackness
marches on.

The huge, the pungent object of our prime out-ride
is to Comprehend,
to salute and to Love the fact that we are Black,
which *is* our "ultimate Reality,"
which is the lone ground
from which our meaningful metamorphosis,
from which our prosperous staccato,
group or individual, can rise.

Self-shriveled Blacks.
Begin with gaunt and marvelous concession:
YOU are our costume and our fundamental bone.

All of you—
you COLORED ones,
you NEGRO ones,
those of you who proudly cry
"I'm half INDian"—
those of you who proudly screech
"I'VE got the blood of George WASHington in
MY veins—
ALL of you—
you proper Blacks,
you half-Blacks,
you wish-I-weren't Blacks,
Niggeroes and Niggerenes.

You.

To Those of My Sisters Who Kept Their Naturals

Never to look a hot comb in the teeth.

Sisters!
I love you.
Because you love you.
Because you are erect.
Because you are also bent.
In season, stern, kind.
Crisp, soft—in season.
And you withhold.
And you extend.

And you Step out.
And you go back.
And you extend again.
Your eyes, loud-soft, with crying and with smiles,
are older than a million years.
And they are young.
You reach, in season.
You subside, in season.
And All
below the richrough righttime of your hair.

You have not bought Blondine.
You have not hailed the hot-comb recently.
You never worshiped Marilyn Monroe.
You say: Farrah's hair is hers.
You have not wanted to be white.
Nor have you testified to adoration of that state
with the advertisement of imitation
(*never* successful because the hot-comb is laughing too.)

But oh the rough dark Other music!
the Real,
the Right.
The natural Respect of Self and Seal!
          Sisters!
Your hair is Celebration in the world!

The Near-Johannesburg Boy

In South Africa the Black children ask each other: "Have you been detained yet? How many times have you been detained?"

———

The herein boy does not live in Johannesburg. He is not allowed to live there. Perhaps he lives in Soweto.

My way is from woe to wonder.
A Black boy near Johannesburg, hot
in the Hot Time.

Those people
do not like Black among the colors.
They do not like our
calling our country ours.
They say our country is not ours.

Those people.
Visiting the world as I visit the world.
Those people.
Their bleach is puckered and cruel.

It is work to speak of my Father. My Father.
His body was whole till they Stopped it.
Suddenly.
With a short shot.

But, before that, physically tall and among us,
he died every day. Every moment.
My Father . . . .
First was the crumpling.

No. First was the Fist-and-the-Fury.
Last was the crumpling. It is
a little used rag that is Under, it is not,
it is not my Father gone down.

About my Mother. My Mother
was this loud laugher
below the sunshine, below the starlight at festival.
My Mother is still this loud laugher!
Still moving straight in the Getting-It-Done (as she
    names it.)
Oh a strong eye is my Mother.
Except when it seems we are lax in our looking.

Well, enough of slump, enough of Old Story.
Like a clean spear of fire
I am moving. I am not still. I am ready
to be ready.
I shall flail
in the Hot Time.

Tonight I walk with
a hundred of playmates to where
the hurt Black of our skin is forbidden.
There, in the dark that is our dark, there,
a-pulse across earth that is our earth, there,

there exulting, there Exactly, there redeeming, there
    Roaring Up
(oh my Father)
we shall forge with the Fist-and-the-Fury:
we shall flail in the Hot Time:
we shall
we shall

Shorthand Possible

A long marriage makes shorthand possible.
The Everything need not be said.
Much may stay within the head.
Because of old-time double-seeing.
Because of old-time double-being.

The early answer answers late.
So comfortably out-of-date.

The aged photographs come clear.
To dazzle down the now-and-here.

I said: "Some day we'll have Franciscan China."
You said: "Some day the Defender will photograph your
    house."
You said: "I want you to have at least two children."

Infirm

Everybody here
is infirm.
Everybody here is infirm.
Oh. Mend me. Mend me. Lord.

Today I
say to them
say to them
say to them, Lord:
look! I am beautiful, beautiful with
my wing that is wounded
my eye that is bonded
or my ear not funded
or my walk all a-wobble.
I'm enough to be beautiful.

You are
beautiful too.

The Coora Flower

Tinsel Marie

Today I learned the *coora* flower
grows high in the mountains of Itty-go-luba Bésa.
Province Meechee.
Pop. 39.

Now I am coming home.
This, at least, is Real, and what I know.

It was restful, learning nothing necessary.
School is tiny vacation. At least you can sleep.
At least you can think of love or feeling your boy friend
       against you
(which is not free from grief.)

But now it's Real Business.
I am Coming Home.

My mother will be screaming in an almost dirty dress.
The crack is gone. So a Man will be in the house.

I must watch myself.
I must not dare to sleep.

Nineteen Cows in a Slow Line Walking

Jamal

When I was five years old
I was on a train.
From a train window I saw
nineteen cows in a slow line walking.

Each cow was behind a friend.
Except for the first cow,
who was God.

I smiled until
one cow near the end
jumped in front of a friend.

That reminded me of my mother and of my father.
It spelled what is their Together.

I was sorry for the spelling lesson.

I turned my face from the glass.

I Am A Black

Kojo

According to my Teachers,
I am now an African-American.

They call me out of my name.

BLACK is an open umbrella.
I am Black and A Black forever.

I am one of The Blacks.

We are Here, we are There.
We occur in Brazil, in Nigeria, Ghana,
in Botswana, Tanzania, in Kenya,
in Russia, Australia, in Haiti, Soweto,
in Grenada, in Cuba, in Panama, Libya,
in England and Italy, France.

We are graces in any places.
I am Black and A Black
forever.

I am other than Hyphenation.

I say, proudly, MY PEOPLE!
I say, proudly, OUR PEOPLE!

Our People do not disdain to eat yams or melons or
      grits
or to put peanut butter in stew.

I am Kojo. In West Afrika Kojo
means Unconquerable. My parents
named me the seventh day from my birth
in Black spirit, Black faith, Black communion.
I am Kojo. I am A Black.
And I Capitalize my name.

Do not call me out of my name.

Uncle Seagram

Merle

My uncle likes me too much.

I am five and a half years old, and in kindergarten.
In kindergarten everything is clean.

My uncle is six feet tall with seven bumps on his chin.
My uncle is six feet tall, and he stumbles.
He stumbles because of his Wonderful Medicine
packed in his pocket all times.

Family is ma and pa and my uncle,
three brothers, three sisters, and me.

Every night at my house we play checkers and
    dominoes.
My uncle sits *close*.
There aren't any shoes or socks on his feet.
Under the table a big toe tickles my ankle.
Under the oilcloth his thin knee beats into mine.
And mashes. And mashes.

When we look at TV
my uncle picks *me* to sit on his lap.
As I sit, he gets hard in the middle.
I squirm, but he keeps me, and kisses my ear.

I am not even a girl.

Once, when I went to the bathroom,
my uncle noticed, came in, shut the door,
put his long white tongue in my ear,
and whispered "We're Best Friends, and Family,
and we know how to keep Secrets."

My uncle likes me too much. I am worried.

I do not like my uncle anymore.

Abruptly

Buchanan

God is a gorilla.

I see him standing in the sky.
He is clouds.
There's a beard that is
white and light gray.

His arms are gorilla arms,
limp at his sides; his fists
not easy but not angry.

I tell my friend.
Pointing, I tell my friend
"God is a gorilla. Look!
There!"

My friend says "It is a crime
to call God a gorilla. You have insulted our God."

I answer:
"Gorilla is majesty.
Other gorillas
know."

An Old Black Woman, Homeless, and Indistinct

1.

Your every day is a pilgrimage.
A blue hubbub.
Your days are collected bacchanals of fear and self-
     troubling.

And your nights! Your nights.
When you put you down in alley or cardboard or
     viaduct,
your lovers are rats, finding your secret places.

2.

When you rise in another morning,
you hit the street, your incessant enemy.

See? Here you are, in the so-busy world.
You walk. You walk.
You pass The People.
No. The People pass you.

Here's a Rich Girl marching briskly to her charms.
She is suede and scarf and belting and perfume.

She sees you not, she sees you very well.
At five in the afternoon Miss Rich Girl will go Home
to brooms and vacuum cleaner and carpeting,
two cats, two marble-top tables, two telephones,
shiny green peppers, flowers in impudent vases, visitors.
Before all that there's luncheon to be known.
Lasagna, lobster salad, sandwiches.
All day there's coffee to be loved.
There are luxuries
of minor dissatisfaction, luxuries of Plan.

3.

That's her story,
You're going to vanish, not necessarily nicely, fairly soon,
Although essentially dignity itself a death
is not necessarily tidy, modest or discreet.
When they find you
your legs may not be tidy nor aligned.
Your mouth may be all crooked or destroyed.

Black old woman, homeless, indistinct—
Your last and least adventure is Review.
    Folks used to celebrate your birthday!
Folks used to say "She's such a pretty little thing!"
Folks used to say "She draws such handsome horses,
    cows and houses,"
Folks used to say "That child is going far."

September, 1992.

BIOGRAPHICAL NOTE

Gwendolyn Brooks was born in Topeka, Kansas, on June 7, 1917. She was raised in Chicago, where her parents—Keziah Corinne Wims Brooks, a teacher, and David Anderson Brooks, a janitor—had moved while she was an infant. She graduated from Englewood High School in 1934, and from Wilson Junior College, where she majored in English literature, in 1936. While pursuing her studies, she became a regular contributor of poetry and prose to "Lights and Shadows," a column in the weekly *Chicago Defender*. She hoped unsuccessfully to join the *Defender* staff as a reporter, working instead at a number of odd jobs and eventually as publicity director for the NAACP Youth Council. She married Henry L. Blakely, a writer, in 1939, and had a son, Henry, in 1940 (her daughter, Nora, was born in 1951). In the early 1940s, she began to publish poetry in national magazines such as *Harper's*, *Poetry*, and the *Saturday Review of Literature*; her first book, *A Street in Bronzeville*, appeared in 1945. She was awarded Guggenheim fellowships in 1946 and 1947. Her second collection of poetry, *Annie Allen* (1949), won the Pulitzer Prize for Poetry. Her first and only novel, *Maud Martha* (1953), was followed by *Bronzeville Girls and Boys* (1956), *The Bean Eaters* (1960), and *Selected Poems*

(1963). She began a career as a professor of poetry in 1963, at Columbia College in Chicago, and later taught at the University of Wisconsin-Madison, the City College of New York, Northeastern Illinois University, and Chicago State University. In 1968, after the death of Carl Sandburg, she was named poet laureate of Illinois. Her later poetry collections include *In the Mecca* (1968), *Riot* (1969), *Family Pictures* (1970), *Beckonings* (1975), *Primer for Blacks* (1980), *The Near-Johannesburg Boy* (1986), *Gottschalk and the Grand Tarantelle* (1988), and *Children Coming Home* (1991); she also edited a number of books, including *Jump Bad: A New Chicago Anthology* (1971), and wrote two volumes of autobiography: *Report from Part One* (1972) and *Report from Part Two* (1996). In 1985–86, she served as Consultant in Poetry, the unofficial poet laureate, at the Library of Congress; in 1995 she won the National Medal of Arts. She died of cancer on December 3, 2000, at her home in Chicago.

NOTE ON THE TEXTS

The poems in this volume are presented in the order in which they first appeared in one of Gwendolyn Brooks's books; some had been published earlier in periodical form, and some were republished—without revision, generally—in one or more collections of her poetry. The texts have been taken from the first printings, listed below:

A Street in Bronzeville. New York: Harper & Brothers, 1945.
Annie Allen. New York: Harper & Brothers, 1949.
The Bean Eaters. New York: Harper & Brothers, 1960.
Selected Poems. New York: Harper & Row, 1963.
In the Mecca. New York: Harper & Row, 1968.
Riot. Detroit: Broadside Press, 1969.
Family Pictures. Detroit: Broadside Press, 1970.
Beckonings. Detroit: Broadside Press, 1975.
Primer for Blacks. Chicago: Brooks Press, 1980.
The Near-Johannesburg Boy, and Other Poems. Chicago: The David Company, 1986.
Children Coming Home. Chicago: The David Company, 1991.
In Montgomery, and Other Poems. Chicago: Third World Press, 2003.

The texts of the original printings chosen for inclusion here are presented without change, except for the correction of typographical errors. Spelling, punctuation, and capitalization are often expressive features and are not altered, even when inconsistent or irregular. Two errors have been corrected: 10.16, inclination.); 108.26, Well—.

NOTES

16.10   *Dorie Miller*] Dorie Miller (1919–1943), who served as ship's cook, third class, on the battleship *West Virginia*, was awarded the Navy Cross for his actions during the Japanese attack on Pearl Harbor. He was killed in the sinking of the escort carrier *Liscome Bay* in the Gilbert Islands.

35.5–7   "*pygmies* . . . YOUNG] From Young's *Night Thoughts* (1742–46): "Pygmies are pygmies still, though percht on Alps; / And pyramids are pyramids in vales. / Each man makes his own stature, builds himself. / Virtue alone outbuilds the Pyramids; / Her monuments shall last when Egypt's fall."

68.2   Emmett Till] Till, a 14-year-old African-American boy from Chicago, was beaten and shot to death in Tallahatchie County, Mississippi, on August 28, 1955, after he allegedly whistled at a white woman; the two white men charged with the crime were acquitted on September 23.

90.9   *Dudley Randall*] Poet (b. 1914) and founder of Broadside Press.

92.7   *Edward Christmas*] Chicago-based flutist and composer.

93.2   Phil Cohran] Chicago-based trumpeter and composer who played with the Sun Ra Arkestra in the late 1950s and was a founder of the AACM.

94.5   Blackstone Rangers] Chicago street gang founded in the early 1960s; it established branches in other cities and was later known variously as the Black P. Stone Nation and El Rukns.

97.4   RON KARENGA]   Black nationalist organizer (b. 1941) who founded the group US in the 1960s.

98.2   *Walter Bradford*]   Writer associated with the Chicago group Organization of Black American Culture, founded in 1967.

100.21   *"Que tu es grossier!"*]   "How crude you are!"

102.21–22   Melvin Van Peebles . . . Lillie . . . Zampoughi]   "Lilly Done the Zampoughi Every Time I Pulled Her Coattail," song by Melvin Van Peebles from his theatrical work *Ain't Supposed to Die a Natural Death* (1971).

103.6   Young-Holt]   Young-Holt Unlimited, a Chicago-based instrumental group founded by members of the Ramsey Lewis Trio, had a number of hit records including "Wack Wack" (1967) and "Soulful Strut" (1968).

116.2   *Al Green*]   Soul singer who enjoyed great success beginning in the early 1970s; his records included "I'm Still in Love with You" and "Let's Stay Together."

121.14   Farrah's hair]   Farrah Fawcett (b. 1947), sometimes known as Farrah Fawcett-Majors, star of the television series *Charlie's Angels* in its first season, 1976–77, was known for her elaborate and widely imitated hairstyle.

INDEX OF TITLES
AND FIRST LINES

ABOUT THIS SERIES

The American Poets Project offers, for the first time in our history, a compact national library of American poetry. Selected and introduced by distinguished poets and scholars, elegant in design and textually authoritative, the series will make widely available the full scope of our poetic heritage.

ABOUT THE PUBLISHER

The Library of America, a nonprofit publisher, is dedicated to preserving America's best and most significant writing in handsome, enduring volumes, featuring authoritative texts.